'You've found happiness with someone else?'

Katy considered lying, but truth was too important to her.

'I've found a life I enjoy, work I love and contentment, Jake. I was never the risk-taker you were,' she said. 'And that hasn't changed.'

'So, going out with me again, even on an "old friends" basis, would be a risk?' he challenged, his voice full of teasing laughter, as if all his doubts had suddenly been banished.

She tried to work out what she'd said to change his mood, but couldn't find an answer. The temptation to say yes was so strong she felt her lips moving. Then she remembered Julia.

Having pursued many careers—from school-teaching to pig-farming—with varying degrees of success and plenty of enjoyment, **Meredith Webber** seized on the arrival of a computer in her house as an excuse to turn to what had always been a secret urge—writing. As she had more doctors and nurses in the family than any other professional people, the medical romance seemed the way to go! Meredith lives on the Gold Coast of Queensland in Australia, with her husband and teenage son.

Recent titles by the same author:

A FATHER FOR CHRISTMAS

TO DR CARTWRIGHT,
A DAUGHTER

BY
MEREDITH WEBBER

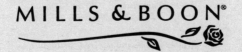

MILLS & BOON®

First published in Great Britain 1998
Harlequin Mills & Boon Limited,
Eton House, 18-24 Paradise Road, Richmond, Surrey TW9 1SR

© Meredith Webber 1998

ISBN 0 263 80731 2

Set in Times Roman 10½ on 12 pt.
91-9802-50244 C1

Printed and bound in Great Britain

CHAPTER ONE

'HI, GANG! We're back!'

Katy grinned as the children playing in the brightly decorated hospital crèche turned as one, then advanced on Julia with loud cries of greeting and delight. Her heart tripped a beat as she watched Julia's special friend seize her hand and hurry her towards the far corner of the room.

'Come and see what I've made,' he urged, skipping in his haste to 'show' his friend the tower of blocks. 'Look!'

He dragged at her arm until her fingers could touch the vinyl tiles. 'See, there's the floor, and here's my tower. It's a look-out for the castle I'm going to build—a castle for a fairy princess.'

'I know he's an unlikely candidate for a prince,' Nan Chalmers, director of Lake Shore North's childcare service, remarked as she joined Katy in the front entrance to the room. 'But he knew Julia was due back today, and he's been working on her castle all week.'

Katy looked at the little boy, already rumpled and grubby-looking, although she knew he'd have been shining clean when his father dropped him off earlier this morning. Peter Clarke was one of those children who threw themselves wholeheartedly into whatever they were doing, regardless of dirt, dire consequences, or damage to self and clothing.

'He's been more than a prince to Julia,' Katy murmured, watching as the boy guided her daughter's fingers up the intricate tower of blocks. 'Peter's a natural leader, and when he accepted Julia without reservations, the other kids knew it was okay to be her friend.'

She saw Nan nod, then shake her head.

'It might have helped,' the director argued, explaining her contradictory reaction, 'but Julia's own nature would have won through even without Peter. I've rarely had to deal with so fearless a child, and other children admire that kind of spirit.'

Katy felt the words tug at the strings which bound her to her child. A fearless sighted child would be bad enough, but for her visually impaired daughter to have inherited her father's reckless streak was something she was trying to ignore.

'So, how was the holiday? You're very brown, and so relaxed you're almost shining. Or is the shine to do with something else? Has John popped the question?'

Nan's words jolted Katy out of the past. It was a long time since she'd thought of Julia's father—since she'd allowed herself to think of him! Yet, she'd slipped back so far—and so quickly—it took her a moment to place John.

'To answer the last question first, no, he hasn't—and even if he had, I'd have said no! I don't love him, Nan. I know he's kind, and good with Julia, and he'd probably make a perfect husband, but...'

'No buzz, huh?' her friend asked, and Katy shook her head.

Definitely no buzz—not that she was looking for the 'buzzing' kind of love.

'We're too different,' she began, trying to explain the idea which had started to crystallise during the month at the beach. 'I mean, on holiday I'm the ultimate slob. I dig in the sand, swim, walk a bit, sleep in the afternoon and eat fish and chips rather than cook.'

'Sounds perfect to me,' Nan sighed.

Katy smiled at her.

'That's why we're friends—both slothful! Anyway, John came up to visit a couple of times and I think he was shocked by such degenerate behaviour. He's more into elegant candle-lit suppers. He seemed to think one shouldn't lower one's standards just because one's at the beach. And the beach bothered him too—so much sand. We've parted, but quite amicably.'

She sighed and shook her head with an undefined regret. He was such a good, steady, reliable man—why couldn't she love him?

'I think he realised it was wrong, too,' she admitted. 'I mean, we've been going around together for six months and haven't progressed past a goodnight kiss. He must have read something into that.'

'I doubt it,' Nan said cryptically, her gaze scanning her friend from top to toe. 'You're looking far too gorgeous for any red-blooded man to resist. Your hair's bleached as light as Julia's and you both tan so well. I can understand Peter wanting her for his princess—'

'And John wanting me for his?' Katy interrupted with a chortle of delighted mirth. 'Sorry, but I'm not cut out to run a castle! Now, if you'll excuse me, I'd better get to work—or the red-blooded male who's taken over the obstetrics department will be firing me on my first day back.'

She whirled across to where Julia was playing, and knelt beside her to kiss her on the cheek.

'See you this afternoon,' she said softly, and Julia's green eyes, so like her own, turned towards her voice.

'Be good, princess!' She touched Peter's reddening cheek and hurried away.

Nan had picked up a toddler and was talking to the child's mother. Katy recognised the woman as the parent of a long-term paediatric patient, and felt a thrill of pride that the crèche she'd fought so hard to establish was being used by both staff and visitors.

'I'll see you later,' she called to Nan, slipping out through the childproof gate that guarded the front entrance.

'I didn't tell you—' her friend called, but she couldn't wait to hear the rest of Nan's news. They could talk this afternoon.

As she walked out of the crèche she paused, as she usually did, to marvel at the transformation the groundsmen had achieved in the last two years. Lake Shore North was a private hospital set in beautiful grounds on the northern end of the lake which gave the city its name.

When the woman who had minded Julia while Katy worked had moved away Katy had begun her campaign for a hospital childcare service. Before tackling the authorities, she'd searched the building for a suitable space and finally found an old storeroom which had looked out over a patch of rough bitumen and three disused incinerators. It had been such an unlikely place to site a crèche her annexing of it had been unopposed.

Now the bitumen had been replaced with grass, and wide sails provided shady areas where the children played. The largest of the incinerators had been cleaned out and converted into a playhouse and the others demolished, their bricks providing the material for the low, zig-zagging balance walls and a creeper-covered mini-maze.

The thrill of pride remained with her as she entered a

side entrance to the building. She hurried along the corridors towards the main foyer of the hospital, nodding greetings to people she knew by sight if not by name. Waiting for the lift to the fourth floor obstetrics wards, she chatted to a nurse who'd just begun her roster in the maternity section.

'Are you enjoying it?' Katy asked, and the girl shrugged.

'It's okay, but I've come from Paediatrics and Dr Gordon is such a sweetie. Copping a perfectionist like this boss straight after him is a bit of a shock. The problem is he simply oozes sex-appeal, so it's almost impossible to keep your mind on the job, then he fires a question at you and—'

'Dan Petersen oozes sex-appeal?' Katy broke in. 'He's nice-looking enough, but sex-appeal? And as for upsetting staff, a more mild-mannered man I have yet to meet.'

'But Dr Petersen didn't take over,' the nurse told her. 'He won some scholarship to study overseas for two months and this Dr Cartwright's filling in.'

The lift arrived and the doors opened.

'Dr Cartwright?' Katy echoed, ignoring more twinges of memory as she tried to place the obstetrician the woman had mentioned.

'At your service!' a deep voice said, and her head jerked upward, shocked into motion by cadences she would never forget. The aforementioned sex-appeal was flowing more freely than an ooze, and Katy could only stare at him, seeing again the slightly uneven balance of his face—craggy features put together in such a way it had a unique attraction—the breadth of his shoulders, the tilt of his head as if he was always listening to something others couldn't hear.

'J-Jake?' she stammered, and watched the lift doors diminish her view of him, so she saw less and less—then finally nothing. She closed her eyes and found the image imprinted on her eyelids. Had he seemed surprised, or had his eyes been laughing at her shock?

'Were you wanting to go up?'

The doors had opened again and he was still there, his face set in a politely enquiring mask. She saw the speculative looks on the faces of staff she knew and spotted the new nurse hovering by his side.

She wasn't trying to get too far away from the sex-appeal, Katy thought bitchily as she stepped into the metal cube.

She had intended finding a corner as far away from Jake Cartwright as the crush of people would allow, but he moved in such a way that the only available space was between him and the nurse.

She wondered if fate might intervene and render her invisible, but fate seemed to be busy elsewhere so she squeezed into the space and breathed in the fresh sharp minty smell of him, a combination of aftershave and toothpaste. She tried to tell herself a lot of people smelled that way.

The lift stopped on 'One' and she was pressed against him as people squeezed their way out and more entered. She could feel the hardness of bone beneath fine wool and muscle and her blood grew hot with embarrassment.

'It's obviously an all-stations,' he said cheerfully, as they were thrust together again on the second floor.

'Change of shifts,' she muttered, battling to overcome the dizzy feeling of faintness swooping through her chest and weakening the bones in her legs. It was more than six years since they'd last met and her body was reacting as if it had been six minutes. Her mind, which should have been producing the neat dismissive speeches she'd practised over those intervening years—practised in the dreams where one day they met again—was paralysed into inactivity.

When the doors opened on 'Four' she practically ran out into the foyer, but, as he followed, she realised there was nowhere to hide. If the nurse was correct, Jake was the new director of obstetrics at Lake Shore North—or the new temporary director.

Which made him her boss!

To make matters worse, as administrative assistant to the director, her desk was in his office—they would be shut away together for at least some part of every day.

She couldn't work with him! Every nerve in her body was screaming its own warning. Could she request a transfer to another department? Immediately?

Would someone swap with her?

She felt his hand close around her arm and turned reluctantly. He would still be in the hospital, she realised, wherever she was working—walking the same corridors, breathing the same air. She gazed at him in despair, noticing the way his hair was touched with grey above one temple—where a scar threaded its way across his skin. The fear she'd felt for him when he'd lain in the hospital, so still for someone who'd always been so active, returned to paralyse her lungs momentarily.

'So we meet again, Katy?' His voice curled around her name in such a familiar way she shivered at the ghosts of yesterday.

'So it seems!'

She blurted out the words, even more unsettled by the all-encompassing scrutiny he was conducting, in full view of the staff passing through the lobby. His eyes, every bit as blue and beautiful as she remembered, took in the sun-streaked hair framing her face, the lemon blouse and vivid yellow skirt she'd chosen because the day was so bright and sunny. His gaze raked her bare tanned legs and lingered on the pale pink-painted toenails peeping out of her raffia sandals, then returned to linger on her face.

'And very nice it is to see you,' he said at last.

'I've got to go to work,' she snapped. 'I can't stand here all day, playing out some grand reunion scene with you.'

'Ah, but you're looking far too lovely to be working—like a sunshiny, toasty-tanned, pink-tipped, yellow daffodil.'

'Still honey-tongued, Jake?' she countered, refusing to be beguiled by his words. 'Well, perhaps you can find someone who'd appreciate your flowery compliments. As I said, I've work to do.'

She turned away from him, heading for her office, then her steps faltered—it was *their* office, not just hers!

It gave him time to catch up with her. To touch her so they paused again.

'Imagine my surprise when they told me my assistant would be one Katherine Anne Turner!' he said, and a tiny flicker of apprehension cut through her confusion. The words rang true—but not entirely. There was something else there, something she couldn't quite fathom.

'You were going to be a nurse, not an office girl,' he added, rubbing at his forehead as if to massage his memory. Recognising his uncertainty in the unconscious movement, she wondered if he was as thrown by this unexpected encounter as she was.

But he'd been at Lake Shore North a week. He knew she worked here and would have been expecting her back from her holiday today.

They were blocking the corridor while her mind tried to assimilate too much information at once and her body struggled to understand she didn't want it reacting to Jake as it had in the past.

He was waiting for an answer. What had he asked her?

'Going to be a nurse?' he prompted helpfully, and she guessed he was concealing his amusement behind his bland façade.

'I was going to be a lot of things. Including, at one stage—if I remember rightly—your wife.'

She hadn't known how bitter she still felt until she heard the cutting edge on the words.

'But that's all in the past!' she added, and shrugged as if to show how unimportant it was.

'Of course,' he said quietly, but his hand dropped from her arm in an involuntary flinch and he turned too quickly to walk away.

With a lurch of pain, she saw a slight unevenness in his stride and wondered how a man who'd taken his physical perfection for granted handled even so mild a disability.

She followed him reluctantly,

Impossible to think they could work together!

She stopped again, knowing her shocked brain couldn't cope with physical and mental processes at the same time—and right now she needed to think more than she needed to walk.

It's only for two months, she reminded herself. That's eight weeks of five days. That's forty days. Wasn't forty days a Biblical measure of time—something about forty days in the wilderness?

The wilderness would be okay—it was the company she couldn't handle!

A muffled giggle hovered on her lips. She must be hysterical!

It's not a joke, she told herself severely, but the still unsteady beating of her heart reminded her she had to get through this next encounter whatever way she could—and if joking was the best way, she would use it. Perhaps that was the answer—perhaps if she could keep it light—act unconcerned?

She hesitated outside Ward 'B', considering a quick visit to the nurses' station to say hello to all the staff. But that would only delay the inevitable, and probably make her next meeting with Jake even more difficult. She thought about resigning, but knew she wouldn't. Julia was settled at the crèche and making friends who would go on with her to the primary school just up the road.

Julia! Her fingers pressed against her lips to stop the name coming out as a despairing cry. Until that moment she hadn't considered her daughter in this strange equation of past and present. But Julia was definitely part of it—the factor 'X', the unknown quantity!

And she'd better stay that way, Katy vowed, closing out the panic which hammered in her head.

Thinking of Julia both sobered and strengthened her. She straightened her shoulders, drew herself up to her full five foot seven, and headed down the passage, telling herself she could handle this—just as she'd handled all the other challenges life had thrown her way.

But how she'd handle it she wasn't certain...

As she pushed open the door to their joint office, she saw he was bent over a filing cabinet in one corner of the room. For a tall man, a fraction over six feet, his movements had a particular grace, so he didn't look awkward or ungainly hunched above the drawer.

'Ah,' he murmured, straightening up and glancing at his watch.

'Don't pull that trick on me, Jake Cartwright!' she snapped, forgetting she'd been going to keep it light. 'This hospital owes me more time off in lieu of overtime than it could ever repay. In fact, if I had any brains I'd take the lot—beginning right now!'

'Running away, Katy?'

The challenge was so softly spoken she barely heard it, but it did serve to stiffen her resolve and helped her cross the distance between the door and her desk—a track that took her dangerously close to Jake.

'You've moved the desks!' The words were startled out of her, and she frowned as she considered his re-arrangement of what she thought of as 'her' office.

The previous director had disliked uneven light, so he had placed his desk in the far corner of the large room. He'd sat facing the door and had grouped the four comfortable visitors' chairs in a horseshoe in front of the desk. Katy had angled her desk on the far side of the room, so she could see the door but also see out of the window and feed her soul with the beauty of the lake in all its moods.

'Why should you be the only one with a view?' he responded easily. 'I think this way will work well.'

Jake had grouped the comfortable chairs around a small coffee table, so visitors could discuss things without the barrier of a wide desk between him and them, then he'd set his desk at an angle to hers. They'd be working an arm's length from each other!

She considered the extra leave she was due—more seriously this time.

'Don't you?'

She didn't have to look at him to know there'd be a

glint of mischief lurking in his eyes. But she wasn't going to let him tease his way back into her heart—then turn away from her again.

'Oh, I'm sure it will,' she agreed, letting sarcasm rip along the words. 'Any time you annoy me, I can pick up the brass pelvic frame a kind medical rep gave me and belt you over the head with it.'

His lips twitched but he didn't smile—which was just as well! A smile might have torn aside her thin veil of composure and left her vulnerable to the full force of his appeal.

'I'd thought of other conveniences,' he said softly. 'After all, if one desk is fun, imagine two!'

The heat began in her toes and fingertips, then raced upward through her body until it was flaring in her cheeks and pulsing in her blood. How dared he remind her of that silly escapade?

And how dared her body remember it so vividly?

'Don't even think about it!' She spaced the words to emphasise the threat. 'I'll work with you for two months, Jake Cartwright, but that is it. If you had some crazy idea of renewing an old relationship—if you fancied I'd melt into a little puddle of desire every time you walked through the door—then forget it! What happened between us was over a long time ago.'

Glaring ferociously at him, she added, 'And it was your choice, remember?'

She flicked at an imaginary bit of dust on her desk, but his next words stabbed into her heart.

'Can *you* forget it?' he asked.

Ignore him! her heart shouted.

'Forget the past, Katy?'

The repetition of the words rasped across her skin,

activating nerve-endings so the hairs on her arms bristled to attention.

She opened her mouth to speak but found she'd forgotten how to form words—even if her brain could think of some to say. Her heart was thumping so loudly she was certain he must be able to hear it.

He was studying her face, her lips. She tried to moisten them but her tongue was also dry and she realised she was breathing through her mouth, dragging air into lungs that laboured in her chest. She knew she had to answer his question or lose this battle before it had begun.

'Most of it,' she lied valiantly.

'But not all?' he persisted. 'Not everything?'

He stepped towards her—one pace, then another, and another, and another—until he stood so close she could see his chest rising and falling as he breathed.

'Not this?'

His voice had changed so the words were velvet-smooth. He raised the back of his hand to the side of her neck, sliding it upward towards her ear, lifting the hair that tumbled to her shoulders and hefting it as if testing its weight. She steeled herself against the touch, against the seduction of his voice and the assault she knew would follow as he bent his head and pressed his lips to hers.

She reminded herself of her little daughter, growing up without a father, and told herself she hated him.

His tongue slid along the line of her mouth, then eased between her lips to touch her teeth. How could one man's kiss rouse the blood to tumult when another's left it cold?

Don't think about him. Don't respond, she ordered her body. Don't move, don't flinch, don't let him guess your heart is battering itself to death. Keep your lips closed and your hands still.

Her fingernails bit into the palms of her hands as she resisted the urge to reach up and touch him, while her lips ached with the need to kiss him back, or to part and allow his kiss to deepen. Then, just as she knew she must give in—must fall against his body and let herself feel the magic one more time—he moved away, deep, half-spoken curses rumbling in his throat.

Katy stepped behind her desk and sank into her chair, pleased she'd made it that far before her trembling legs gave out and betrayed her deceit. She opened the top drawer and pulled out the bits and pieces she usually kept on her desk.

Her handbag went into the bottom drawer, then she found the file of notes Jillian, her temporary replacement, had left for her, and the folder with the information on the new maternity unit.

'I'm sorry, Katy!' he muttered, and crossed to slump down in his own chair—still frowning. 'What I did just now—that was unforgivable.'

Jake apologising? He *had* changed!

'Yes, it was!' she agreed, unwilling to let him off the hook too easily. Then an imp of mischief prompted her to add, 'I certainly wouldn't recommend coming on to all your administrative assistants quite that strongly. Not on the first day, at any rate!'

He growled something that sounded quite profane and she knew she had come out on top in this first encounter. She relaxed a little. If she could hide her own turmoil behind a determinedly professional manner she might just survive the next two months!

Determinedly professional! That was the approach.

And don't even think of Julia in case he can still read your thoughts!

'I assume Jillian introduced you to all the staff and showed you around? You've got the schedules for the month,' she began, seeing the note Jillian had attached to her own copy of the list of meetings he was expected to attend. 'You probably realise you won't make half these meetings because you're on call for emergencies or consultations. So I attend all but the department directors' meetings with you—or without you if you're not available.'

He didn't reply, and when she glanced towards him she realised he probably hadn't heard her. He had a puzzled look on his face, as if he'd turned a corner and found himself in a foreign land.

His abstracted demeanour gave her confidence.

'Actually, I could probably run this office on my own, but the hospital seems to think it needs doctors.' She smiled at the feeble joke, realising she was now far more at ease than he was. Surely that would give her an added advantage!

Then he smiled back, and any advantage she'd thought she had was lost. Her heart fluttered in its beat then lurched into a new staccato rhythm, leaving her breathless.

'Spoken like a true administrator,' he said softly.

She stared at him for a moment, afraid of softness from this man, then she turned her attention back to Jillian's other notes and continued to pretend she was totally unaffected by this cataclysmic reunion.

'There's the monthly ward meeting tomorrow,' she reminded him, glancing up but not quite meeting his eyes. Keep it light, instinct reminded her. Play it as a comedy not a drama.

He seemed uneasy—different from the man she'd encountered earlier in the elevator. Or was she imagining it? The Jake Cartwright she'd known had never had an uneasy moment in his life. Even when he had lain in hospital after those two terrible weeks in Intensive Care he'd been enough in control to tell her she was no longer part of his life.

She put the thought aside and forced herself to concentrate on work.

'Do you have anything in particular you want to discuss? I'll type up an agenda for you.'

There was a long, tight silence, then he muttered something that sounded uncomplimentary to all women and rustled the papers on his own desk. She pretended she hadn't heard and flicked through the rest of the notes Jillian had left for her. Patients were being placed in 'B' and 'C' wings, and 'A' wing should be empty by Wednesday.

Katy nodded at the note. The hospital had been built so these wings could be isolated completely. The original idea had been so the various parts of the hospital could be shut off from each other in case of fire, but it had proved invaluable for cleaning and pest control purposes. The three utility and storage rooms in 'A' wing would have to be emptied tomorrow, then the wing would be ready for its annual steam-clean.

She made a note to check with the ward sister that staff were available to move the supplies out of these rooms. She could call in some extra wardsmen if necessary.

She doodled on the paper, thinking ahead. Because of the chemicals used, it would remain empty for at least a week. And after that...? Counting today and tomorrow, she had nine days to convince Jake that the new maternity unit was a good idea. Could she do it?

She looked up again and this time she did meet his eyes. She even smiled.

'Well, boss,' she said cheekily. 'What shall I put on this agenda of yours?'

CHAPTER TWO

FOR a moment Katy thought she'd gone too far, for Jake's frown deepened, but then he shrugged and opened the folder on his desk.

'Jillian's already drawn up an agenda,' he said, his voice so mild she had to dismiss any idea of uneasiness. In fact, he was now as professionally intent as she was trying to be. 'The only item I don't understand is this new maternity unit. She told me it's your pet project and that you'd explain about it.'

'The new unit—' She'd barely begun when he broke in.

'I should tell you I was told fairly specifically that the hospital can't afford to be spending money. Seems every new department director has a pet project he wants to put into place. When Dan Petersen found he couldn't take up his position immediately, the hospital administration was happy to have me come in because I've made a study of cost analysis in maternity wards. A hospital has to run like any other business. It's expected to pay its way—'

'And make a tidy profit for its shareholders,' Katy interjected as a perverse disappointment swamped her. Jake and cost analysis? It didn't seem possible that the wild, brilliant, people-orientated young man she'd known had become a bean-counter. 'Of course, that's more important than patient satisfaction!' she added bitterly, momentarily forgetting her 'keep it light' decision.

He ignored her sarcasm and continued in a bland tone.

22

'I should also point out that I understood the director's assistant's job was to assist the director, not make snide remarks or instigate changes in the department.'

He sounded so stuffy Katy stared blankly at him for a moment, seeking a sign that he was joking. But no gleam of humour lit his blue eyes! She decided to ignore the jibe and go into attack mode.

'Old Forbes up in the head office has been talking to you. That bit about "paying its way" is exactly what he said to me when the board approved the outlay for the crèche. I fought hard for that crèche, but he can't see past the end of a bank statement where change is concerned. He won't even admit it's a success!'

She pursed her lips, dipped her head, and looked up from under lowered brows to imitate the head accountant.

'"It's not your job to worry about such things, Miss Turner!"' she mimicked in a high-pitched whine, then she grinned to show she meant no malice to the old man.

There was no answering smile.

'Well, how do you see your job?'

Katy felt the smile slide off her lips. Maybe the comedy angle wasn't the answer! Yet how else could she hide the dreadful muddle of emotion and anguish his presence was causing?

Concentrate on work—on the new unit. It was vital to get Jake on side if her wonderful vision was to become a reality. Dan Petersen had approved, but she'd often wondered it he'd have the courage and persistence to fight the money-handlers for it, or convince the consultants and medical staff it would work. Now, Jake, as she remembered him, had loved a challenge. Would bean-counting have changed him?

She couldn't tell by looking at him. He just sat there

at his desk, his eyes fixed on the papers he was shuffling as he waited in silence for her reply.

'Oh, assisting the director, of course,' she murmured, and tried another, more tentative smile. 'Doing whatever is possible to make this department run more smoothly and efficiently, also boosting awareness in the community of the services we offer and promoting the good name of Lake Shore North far and wide.'

His lips twitched, and for a moment she thought he might smile back at her. A hollow feeling in her chest reminded her that his smiling back might not be a good idea, but before she had to worry about it the lips had stilled and his brows had drawn together in a frown. She hurried into speech again.

'At the moment everything is running smoothly in the wards, but our obstetric case numbers are dropping.'

'That's happening everywhere,' he pointed out. 'More people are opting for home births or using small specialist birthing centres—'

'Exactly!' Katy told him, leaping into his opening with her argument. 'And there's no reason why women can't see Lake Shore North as just such a centre.'

'See a fifteen-storey pile of steel and concrete as a "small specialist birthing centre"?' he mocked. 'Are you advocating setting up a cabin in the gardens, or pulling down the building to make way for your brave idea?'

She bit back the retort she'd have liked to make and forced herself to continue calmly.

'There's no reason we can't provide what people want within the confines of this building. It's the feel of the place once people come in that we need to change— what's inside that counts, not the external packaging.'

Vague memories stirred, and she remembered another conversation along the same lines. Jake holding her in front of a darkened shop window, 'See how great we look together!' She'd pulled away and made a similarly pompous little speech. He'd laughed at her, agreeing, but pleased with their reflected image all the same. It hadn't been vanity, with Jake, that had made him pleased about their physical appearance, but part of his need to always seek perfection, to strive to be the fastest, highest, smartest, best!

She glanced up to see him watching her as he waited for her to continue. She couldn't let herself begin to think about the past.

'Lake Shore as a suburb is changing demographically,' she said, looking down at the desk as if she needed to read words she knew by heart. 'The wealthy people who once lived here and chose Lake Shore North to have their babies are moving out to houses on acreage and the old houses in the area are being turned into flats—'

'Which should give us more potential customers, not fewer,' he pointed out. 'I know the hospital has an agreement with the government to take public as well as private patients.'

'Exactly what I keep trying to tell Ol—ah, Mr Forbes,' Katy cut in. 'And we're guaranteed no bad debts with the public patients because the government pays. The problem lies in selling the hospital to the newcomers who would make up the bulk of our public patients.'

'Which, as you've so wisely pointed out, is your job. Can't you do it without spending vast sums of money on a new unit?'

Katy bit her lip and took a deep, steadying breath. In the past, Jake had used such crisp retorts to tempt her into argument, delighting in the cut and thrust as he forced her to validate the point she was making. She had grown to enjoy the verbal sparring, but she suspected shock had numbed her brain too much to win a war of words with him today.

'I'm not suggesting we spend vast sums of money,' she said quietly, homing in on the most valid point in her plan. 'There would be no building costs apart from maybe some repainting, which would come out of the maintenance budget anyway. And no new staffing costs because we will still be operating the same number of beds. At the moment we're over-staffed because we're down on maternity case numbers.'

'So, how does a new unit change things around? What are you advocating—offering women whatever choice they want? Underwater births, pseudo-home births, family rooms, or all of the above?'

He turned away from her before she could reply, staring out of the window towards the lake. It was wind-ruffled today, Katy noticed, with the sun flecking the crests of the tiny waves with gold. She loved the lake in all its moods—a love that had begun when she and Jake had first met and walked beside it...

'You've been here a week; you should know we already offer women those choices. The birthing suites were put in for that purpose, and many women do see them as a valid and acceptable alternative to home birth,' she said, dragging her thoughts resolutely back to the present. 'I'm talking about attitude, about taking into consideration the traditions and feelings of women from other cultures.'

'Other cultures?'

His voice seemed to come from a long way off and his face had lost its sternness when he turned back towards her.

'Particularly Asian cultures,' she said, drawn towards the gleam of interest in his eyes. 'Most of the families shifting into the area are from South-East Asian backgrounds. We have interpreters in the hospital, and we can offer Asian food, but we need to do more in training our staff to understand the ways of these people. And we should have a proper antenatal programme for them, not the hit and miss stuff we're doing now. Also, if we can put the women together in one ward, they will be able to speak to each other and should feel less isolated.'

He moved slightly so he was looking out of the window again, but she knew he was listening—listening to and absorbing her idea. She kept talking—quickly—excited by that spark of interest but knowing he could be called away any minute.

'Grouping them together in one ward would help generate informal support networks for when they leave hospital. These women come from a culture where the family is very involved throughout their pregnancy and confinement, especially the woman's mother and the mother-in-law. Most of our patients are immigrants, having their first babies alone in a foreign country without their traditional family support systems.'

He frowned at her and she wondered what she'd said to annoy him.

'We can't discuss this at the ward meeting tomorrow morning,' he told her, shaking his head as if to dismiss the whole idea.

Katy's temper flared.

'And why not?' she demanded. 'If you're into protocol and doing things by the book, then you have to discuss it because it's on the agenda. The ward staff have all had input into the idea and they're keen to try it, and I've already told you it won't cost your precious shareholders much money. What possible reason could you have for not discussing it tomorrow?'

'Because I know nothing about it?' he responded calmly. 'I can't go into a meeting with only the haziest idea of what we're discussing.'

'I've all the information in here.' She waved the fat file at him. 'Including the number of Asian-born women in the area—taken from the Census—and written information on birthing and confinement customs in South-East Asian countries. It's actually the confinement—'

He held up his hand to stop her flow of words.

'I've a ward round in ten minutes, then appointments scheduled through the day. And judging from the names on the patient list I'll be seeing quite a few of your Asian mothers.'

Katy calmed down enough to explain.

'It's the interpreter's day in our outpatients department. We only have her once a month so we schedule most of the Asian women on the day she's available.'

He frowned again.

'I understood the hospital had a number of interpreters. Why do we only get one once a month?'

Katy let out a little sigh of relief. That ready aggression in his voice told her Jake hadn't lost his fighting spirit.

'On paper we have an interpreter once a week,' she told him. 'The problem is it's a man the other three weeks, and the women won't talk through him. It's hard enough to get them to allow male doctors to examine them, but most of them flatly refuse to discuss personal concerns through a man of their own culture.'

'Do you know this for a fact? Did they tell *you* this?'

He emphasised the 'you', as if puzzled by her involvement. After all, he'd already reminded her that a director's assistant should assist the director, not poke her nose into medical business.

'I keep all the department records on the computer,' she explained. 'In the beginning I noticed a number of women not turning up for appointments and when I chased them up I found out why. Now we try to fit them all in on the day when we have Tan here.'

'When *you* chased them up?' Again he allotted a subtle emphasis to the pronoun.

'I took Tan with me and visited the women,' she explained, and saw the flicker of a grin move the corners of his lips. 'Well, I needed to find out,' she added defensively.

'Of course!' He nodded once, then waited as if he expected her to say more, but that slight lessening of the sternness in his face had made her forget what she was saying.

She couldn't let him defeat her with the ghost of a smile! What had they been discussing before he'd begun to talk about today's appointments?

The agenda!

'So we can discuss this tomorrow?' she asked hopefully.

'Is that all the information you have—that the women won't talk through a male interpreter?'

One eyebrow flicked upwards and she shut her eyes against encroaching memories.

'No, I've a file full of information,' she snapped, banging the folder on top of the table.

'Exactly!' he murmured with maddening control. He stood up and walked across to her desk, lifting the sheaf of papers from her nerveless fingers. 'Information I have to absorb before I can consider its value. I'll try to read through it during the day, but I'll need to discuss it with you once I've read it. Perhaps you could have dinner with me tonight? Staying after work is the only way I can see us making sure the item is included in tomorrow's agenda.'

He tucked the file under his arm and walked out, leaving Katy staring, open-mouthed, at the slowly closing door.

She breathed deeply, trying to ease the tension and confusion battling for supremacy in her body.

You can't still love him after the way he treated you, she reminded herself. This reaction is nothing more than shock with a bit of the old physical stuff thrown in.

The words echoed bravely in her head, but it was the 'old physical stuff' causing most concern. Sweaty palms, palpitations and nausea—actual symptoms unrelated to any medical condition.

She tried deep breathing again, and when that didn't work replayed the scene in this very hospital that was etched so vividly in her mind. She and Jake had worked at Lake Shore General, but he'd been brought here after the accident—after they'd argued over his racing his motorbike! She had told him how much the mountain races frightened her and had begged him to stop, had pleaded with him to ride it for pleasure, if he needed the adrenalin rush bike-riding provided, but not to pit himself against professionals.

She'd refused to go and watch, but she'd felt so sick as she waited for him to come home she might as well have been among the crowd of onlookers scattered down the hillside.

The racing professional who'd become his friend had rung to tell her of the accident, to tell her where the ambulance was headed. It had been the first time she'd been in a private hospital and the wide carpeted corridors and almost silent movement of staff as they went about their business had intimidated her.

But not so much that she'd been cowed—or cowardly!

'I don't believe he said that,' she'd railed at his mother that dreadful day.

His parents had been overseas when it happened and had been difficult to contact, and once they'd arrived Katy had been relegated to an extra in the drama—someone who received information second-hand. 'I want to speak to him myself,' she'd insisted.

And eventually they'd let her.

The colour had come back into his skin since they'd moved him out of the ICU and his eyes had been a darker blue than she'd remembered.

'I asked them not to let you in,' he had said, in a cold voice so unlike his own she'd checked to see it really was Jake lying in the bed.

'Why?' she'd demanded.

'Because it's over, Katy.' He had spoken with a calm deliberation. 'It was over before the accident,' he had added, as if he had needed to hurt her more than she'd already been hurting. 'I think we both knew that.'

There'd been a dreadful pause and she'd realised, for the first time, how silence could hammer in the ears.

'I didn't know it,' she'd managed to mumble, her first priority holding back the encroaching tears. There was no way she'd been going to cry in front of him—or let his parents see her grief!

'Think about it, Katy,' he'd said in that same controlled voice. 'Think about it and you'll find you probably did.'

She had turned and walked away, not even pausing when he called her name.

'Thank you for being there when it happened,' he'd

added, and then she'd spun around, because he'd said the words in a tone in which one thanks a stranger.

'It was nothing,' she'd said with a careless shrug, while her heart had pounded its pain and her lips had trembled with the effort of not screaming out the denial which had ricocheted through her body.

She'd tried to believe it had been the accident, that it had been pain making him behave this way—or perhaps the influence of his parents, who had been with him since he'd been moved out of Intensive Care. But when she'd tried to see him again she'd been refused admittance.

Then his parents had had him transferred to a hospital nearer his home in West Australia and she hadn't seen him again. She had written to him twice, all pride crushed by the pain of his betrayal—and by her own fear of and despair for the future—but the letters had been returned unopened and she had finally accepted he'd meant what he'd said.

'Damn the man!' she muttered to herself, staring out towards the lake through a haze of unshed tears.

The little replay had upset her more than it had armoured her.

Relationships ended—falling out of love was as much a fact of life as falling into it. She'd finally accepted that that was what had happened with Jake, finally decided that the argument they'd had before he'd ridden off and nearly killed himself had been a sign that things were over.

For him, perhaps!

It was just a shame she hadn't felt the same way— that they couldn't have parted at some point where the bloom had rubbed off love for both of them.

'Ms Turner to Ward 'B', please,' her speaker phone requested.

The call was like a lifeline back to safety, and she seized it gratefully, hurrying from the ghosts inhabiting the office.

'We've a Vietnamese patient in early labour and can't contact Tan,' Helen Reynolds, the midwife in charge of Ward 'B', told her. 'Dr Spencer tried to examine her but she yelled at him. I sent him out of the birthing suite and she let me take her blood pressure and pulse, but she's objecting to the external foetal heart rate monitor and becoming more and more distressed.'

'I'll try to talk to her,' Katy offered, 'but my Vietnamese is fairly basic. If she understands Chinese, we'll be right.'

She turned and followed the older woman towards the birthing suites, mentally rehearsing the few Vietnamese words she'd picked up in her first lessons.

When she entered the room, the woman was turned away from her. She was so slight and fragile-looking she might have been a child play-acting with a pillow tucked under her gown. Katy could see the shiny knobs of her spine where the hospital gown gaped at the back and made a mental note to find out about the clothing Asian women wore to give birth. Surely not these practical but embarrassing and unflattering gowns the hospital provided for its patients.

'*Chào bà,*' she said, using the traditional greeting to a woman on their first meeting. She'd have liked to add that it was a lovely day to bring a child into the world, but her knowledge of the language was too limited for flowery speeches.

'We need to know when the pains began and where they are.' The deep voice made Katy spin around to see

Jake standing in the shadows near the door. At least he'd had enough sense to keep out of the patient's line of sight.

The woman screamed, apparently alarmed by the sound of his voice, and curled into a tighter ball on the bed. Katy found the movement puzzling. Apart from anything else, it must be uncomfortable to lie that way. Behind her, Helen murmured to Jake, explaining that most of their Asian patients were extremely stoical during childbirth, the Vietnamese women in particular.

Katy sat on the bed and took the woman's hand. Aware of her limitations in Vietnamese, she spoke quietly to her in Chinese and heard a faint response. She spoke again, and felt the waif-like figure relax. When the next contraction began, the woman squeezed Katy's fingers but she didn't scream.

'Try now,' Helen suggested quietly, and Katy asked the questions.

The woman replied quite calmly and Katy translated for Jake, but when Helen approached with the monitor the dreadful keening cry began again.

One word was repeated over and over, but Katy didn't recognise it. She waved Helen away and spoke again in Chinese, repeating meaningless phrases about relaxing, about trying to be calm so the baby wouldn't be upset.

Something buzzed in Katy's brain. She'd read so much about these immigrant women since she'd begun to investigate the feasibility of the special unit that at first she couldn't isolate the thought. She continued talking quietly in Chinese and massaging the woman's hand with her fingers. It was to do with the past...

Memories of her own pain when she'd experienced the flashback of Jake's rejection provided the clue.

When the next contraction finished, she signalled to a

nurse to take her place beside the woman and motioned to Helen and Jake to follow her outside.

'I read a paper on subconscious memory in women from war-torn countries. Although many of the Asian women in this area came out to join family or fiancés, others were refugees who escaped from persecution. Some of them have lived in dreadful conditions in refugee camps for many years while others have experienced torture or saw their parents tortured—'

'So you think instruments we use—say something as innocuous to us as an external foetal heart monitor with wires from the patient to a machine—could bring back memories and even duplicate the pain?'

It was Jake who caught up her vague idea and took it one step further. She could feel his interest quickening and felt a surge of excitement, but before she could speak again he had turned to Helen.

'Take the monitor screen out of the room,' he suggested. 'And anything else that looks harsh or metallic.'

Helen hurried back into the room, and Katy was about to follow when his hand restrained her.

'What else?' he demanded.

She visualised her notes on the new unit and mentally flipped through to the section she'd put together on Vietnamese women.

'The husband isn't present at the birth,' she said. 'It's definitely women's business.'

'Then midwives should handle her,' Jake agreed. 'I'll tell Ron Spencer to keep out, and stay clear myself unless there's an emergency. Will you talk to her while Helen examines her? Can you stay with her until we track down the interpreter?'

He was treating her as a colleague and she responded accordingly. Her heart might still be aching for the magic of the past, but her mind was fully focused on the young woman in the birthing suite.

'At least he's seen at first hand some of the problems we have,' Helen remarked as Katy returned to the patient. 'That should help our push for the special unit.'

While Katy explained to the fearful woman that they needed to know if the baby was close, Helen took the woman's pulse and gently palpated the distended abdomen. Katy knew from her own pregnancy these were Leopold Manoeuvres, and she tried to convey the idea that Helen was checking the exact position of the baby.

'I need to listen to the foetal heart rate after the next contraction,' Helen said quietly. 'Could you tell her I'll use this foetoscope? If she's attended any antenatal appointments she'll be familiar with it, or with an ordinary stethoscope.'

Katy translated falteringly, using her hands and body language to try to explain the technicalities. She was relieved when the woman touched the instrument and nodded. She watched as Helen moved the cone of the instrument over her belly and smiled when the nursing sister nodded reassuringly.

'Ask her if I can take her blood pressure again now. Explain we need to know how her heart is behaving.'

Again Katy translated, pointing to the sphygmomanometer Helen produced from a cupboard.

The patient seemed to withdraw, then flinched as another contraction gripped her belly. When it subsided, Katy mimed putting on a blood pressure cuff and pumping it tight, and the woman spoke freely for the first time.

'Her doctor used the same thing during her antenatal visits,' Katy told Helen, but when she asked the woman for the name of her doctor, the reply was unfamiliar.

'Asian doctor, not Western doctor,' the woman expanded.

'Do you want this doctor with you?' Katy asked, wondering if there were local Asian GPs she might be able to co-opt into her unit.

The woman giggled shyly, and shook her head.

'He man!' she said in English.

The door opened and Tan appeared, bowing slightly to her colleagues before greeting the woman.

They talked for a few minutes, but Katy couldn't follow the fast-paced conversation.

'Can you stay with her, Katy?' Tan asked. 'I've got to sit in on the outpatient appointments with the new boss.'

'I'll stay,' Katy promised, ignoring thoughts of the paperwork and messages she knew would be multiplying on her desk.

The baby arrived three hours later. Helen delivered him and held him so the mother could see the mucus being wiped from his mouth and nose. A Vietnamese midwife who had worked at Lake Shore North the previous year had told them this was important to her people. 'We believe it prevents asthma or emphysema later on,' she'd explained.

Katy waited until the mother had been gently sponged in warm water, then she helped her dress. She watched the woman wrap layers of clothing around herself, then pull a scarf around her head and warm socks on her feet. She shuddered to think how hot their patient must feel, but she knew it was a custom followed in most Asian countries to heat the body after childbirth.

The tiny boy was checked and weighed, then warmly wrapped and presented to his mother. Her eyes were round with wonderment and she sniffed his skin and smiled. Helen grinned at Katy and made a little thumbs-up sign. The maternity ward had already developed the practise of putting ginger root in the water for bathing Vietnamese babies.

'Can you leave her in this room?' Katy asked, and Helen nodded.

'For the moment we can. I've two other suites available for new admissions. Would you ask her if she wants a meal, and, if so, what she'd like to eat?'

Katy spoke to the woman again.

'Hot foods,' she said to Helen. 'The kitchens have a list of what constitutes ''hot'' and ''cold'' in this context. If nothing else is available at the moment, she'd be happy with salted rice.'

Helen hurried away and Katy explained to the woman that she must also go. She pushed the baby's crib close to the bed.

'The nurse will stay for a while and she will call me if you need anything. Can I phone your husband or a friend?' she asked.

'My husband is in the big entrance place downstairs,' the woman told her in Chinese. 'He brought me here but could not come up to where babies are born.'

CHAPTER THREE

KATY found the new father—easily isolating him as the nervously pacing young man just inside the front door. He was dressed in a pale grey suit and had a rolled black umbrella hooked over one arm. For a moment she was struck by the incongruity of the couple—the man having adopted such formal European dress while upstairs his wife was swaddled in the clothing her female forebears had worn for thousands of years.

She introduced herself and gave him the good news. His dark eyes gleamed like black onyx and his lips tilted up in a smile that would have taken sandpaper to remove.

He told her his name: Nguyen—the Vietnamese equivalent of Smith it was so common—and she suggested they go back up to the fourth floor where he could see his wife and child. After the struggle to communicate with his wife, she was surprised to find he spoke precise, unaccented English.

'I grew up here,' he explained as they waited for the elevator. 'My wife is Vietnamese-born and was chosen by my grandparents in Vietnam. She was sent out when she was old enough to marry. We had corresponded, of course, but as we learned to know each other our love flourished like roses in a garden. She is learning English, but it is difficult for her.'

Katy was smiling at his flowery tribute when the lift arrived, and once again, as the doors opened, she was confronted by Jake. Her heart reacted skittishly, but her head took control. She introduced Mr Nguyen and explained he was now the father of a fine son.

Jake congratulated him, but he seemed detached. Had his session in Outpatients gone badly?

Katy tried to ignore him, although the restricted space and her physical reactions made this feat difficult. She concentrated on practical matters, turning to the new father.

'Can you stay with your wife for the rest of the day?' she asked him, aware that most Vietnamese were unwilling to take time off work, even for the birth of a baby.

'I have taken paternity leave,' he said proudly. 'I teach in a high school and the system allows me one month without pay. It is more important for my wife to have someone to help her while she does the month than for me to be earning money.'

'That's wonderful,' Katy told him as they all stepped out on the fourth floor. 'And if you can be here as much as possible while she is in hospital, you can explain her needs to the nursing staff and doctors. It will mean we don't have to find a translator every time she is examined, and it could save her from possible embarrassment.'

She showed him into the room and left him with his wife and son, only too aware that Jake was hovering behind her.

'"Does the month?"' he queried as they walked back towards their office.

'It's in the notes,' she told him. 'Although a month is common in many countries, originally in Vietnam the postnatal confinement time was one hundred days. Traditionally, there's a One Hundred Day party, when the child is introduced to friends and family.'

'I haven't a clue what you're babbling on about,' he said crossly, 'and I very much doubt I'll have time to read the notes. I've had a harrowing morning in Outpatients, examining pregnant women by remote control, with some of them unwilling even to supply a specimen of urine, let alone blood! And why I'd need an interpreter when half of them refuse to ask questions, pretending they know everything there is to know, yet looking so fearful and puzzled you'd think I was the devil incarnate...'

His voice trailed away, as if the frustration of the morning was too upsetting to recall.

'Specimens are a problem, as some South-East Asian people are reluctant to give strangers any of their body fluids,' Katy explained. She paused and he halted beside her. 'And Cambodian women in particular hold doctors in such high esteem they're reluctant to bother such great men with questions.'

Her lips twitched with delight as she dropped this little gem of information.

He eyed her suspiciously, aware of the mockery in her voice.

'Go on,' he growled.

'Well, it's because of such wide-ranging beliefs and customs we believe the new unit is so necessary. If we can start with group sessions and interpreters in antenatal clinics, we can explain in the women's own language why we use certain procedures—like taking their blood and urine or performing scans—and let them tell us why they do it differently and what practices they find offensive—'

'Offensive?' he echoed.

'Both sides are offended at times,' she told him. 'The women by some of our ways and our staff by some of theirs. If we can begin to educate them in our system, and learn something of their customs and beliefs well before the actual birth, it should be easier to chart a course for their pregnancy and confinement.'

His pager buzzed and he groaned.

'I'm only here for two months, Katy,' he grumbled. 'Couldn't you put your unit on hold until Dan returns?'

'Once you revelled in a challenge,' she reminded him, and saw a shadow darken his cheeks.

'Once I revelled in a lot of things,' he muttered at her, and walked on down the corridor.

He was on the phone when she entered their office. She'd been called back by Helen to discuss a time for the basic Chinese lessons she'd offered to give the staff. Learning the common courtesies in the patients' language was all part of her grand plan!

As she slipped into her seat she saw the 'New Unit' file open on his desk. Had he read it? She tried not to let her hopes rise too high. A consultant director spent so little time in his office—there was always someone wanting his attention. She sat down and began to respond to the messages on her own desk.

They ranged from leaking taps in shower cubicles to an under-supply of the new muslin nappies they were trialling in the nursery. One by one she dealt with these 'housekeeping' matters, concentrating fiercely in an effort to ignore Jake's presence in the room.

'I'm going back down to Outpatients,' he announced when his phone conversation concluded. 'Page me there if you need me.'

Then her phone rang, and he hesitated by her desk while she answered it.

'The director is busy at the moment,' she said, when the voice on the other end paused for breath. 'Dr Spencer

will be doing afternoon ward rounds—' she glanced at
her watch. Could it really be that late? What had happened to lunch? '—any minute. You could ask him
about the problem.'

She listened to the indignation squawk through the
phone. Jake was still hovering on the other side of her
desk. She waved her hand to show him everything was
under control, but he didn't move.

'It's natural to have difficulties at first,' she assured
the distressed patient, 'but I think you'll find the nursing
staff far more helpful than the doctor in this matter.
Many of them have had children themselves and have
experienced the same problems. If Sister has suggested
a mild analgesic you can be certain it will be something
which won't affect your milk or harm the baby.'

She listened quietly, aware the woman on the other
end was regaining her self-control.

'I think the recommended time is forty minutes before
each feed, but timing is difficult if you're demand-
feeding the baby,' she agreed. 'If you're really against
the analgesic, you'd have to put up with the pain. I know
it's uncomfortable, but it's a sign your uterus is contracting and getting back into its pre-pregnancy shape.'

Jake had settled himself to wait out the conversation,
one hip hitched onto the edge of the desk. He was too
close, Katy realised as she continued to soothe the patient. She could see the shape of his thigh muscles
against the material of his suit and found she didn't want
to think about Jake's thigh muscles. Didn't want to think
about any part of Jake!

'If I'd known you weren't busy I'd have sent you
down to see her,' she said tartly when the conversation
had finally come to an end and she'd replaced the receiver. 'I thought you had appointments in Outpatients.'

'An appointment,' he corrected calmly, shifting slightly so she could envisage more muscled thigh beneath the fine grey fabric. 'It's with the head of the interpreters. He'll be working and will fit me in between patients whenever I get there. Do you field all my calls with such expertise?'

She looked up, trying to gauge his mood from his face, but it was expressionless—remote.

'I try to shield the director from unnecessary complications,' she replied primly. 'That's why calls like that come through to me, not you. Mrs Preston is a patient in Ward 'C'. She's having severe after-pains from contractions when she breast feeds, but—'

'Was concerned over analgesia contaminating her breast milk,' he finished. 'I'm an obstetrician; I gathered that much.'

Katy nodded, ignoring the sarcasm. His closeness was making her breathless, as if he'd drawn all the available air out of the room.

'And nurses are more helpful than doctors?' he pursued softly. 'I know you told me I was redundant earlier, but do you always tell the patients how useless we medicos are?'

She felt a ripple of apprehension. Was he annoyed or merely teasing?

'Of course not,' she said, her eyes defying him to argue. 'I was merely pointing out that the nurses have more experience in some fields—and that includes, strangely enough, nursing care!'

'Did you finish your nursing training?'

The question was so unexpected she knew her involuntary jolt of shock must have been visible to him. No matter how much she loved her present job, she couldn't hold back the spurt of regret that she'd failed to complete her degree.

'No,' she admitted quietly.

'Why?'

She closed her eyes to the image of Julia. Her heart was wrenched with pain. Whatever happens, he mustn't know about Julia.

'I had other things to do,' she muttered.

'Like what?'

The question was so harsh she shook her head—responding to the tone not the words.

'So you gave up, just like that?' he mocked, shifting off the desk so he could straighten up and loom over her. 'The fighter who'd sworn she'd make it although it meant working at menial jobs to pay her way and studying through the night?'

He was goading her deliberately, but she couldn't hold back.

'Maybe I lost interest in it,' she challenged. 'Maybe I decided it wasn't what I wanted. You should understand that, Jake,' she reminded him. 'You made the same decision once yourself—about me!'

She reached out and lifted the receiver. The phone hadn't rung, but she needed to look as if she was dismissing him—as if she had more important things to do than argue about their mutual past.

She pressed the memory button for the crèche, aware that he'd taken the hint and was striding towards the door. She was about to respond to Nan's 'hello' when he turned.

'You've made arrangements for tonight?' he asked, and then, without waiting for a reply, he added, 'I've been given a couple of rooms on the top floor. It's the door on the left as you come out of the lift. Come on up when you finish and bring the file. We can order a meal from the kitchen.'

She opened her mouth to object to his orders, but he was gone before she could think of a valid argument—or one that didn't involve mentioning her child.

Was she being foolish? Wouldn't he eventually hear she had a child? It was more than likely! Yet she knew instinctively that Julia must be protected at all costs—must be shielded from the pain he'd inflicted on Katy—that unbearable agony which arose not from love but from the repudiation of it.

She heard a click as the phone in the crèche was disconnected and remembered what she was supposed to be doing. For a moment she considered going down to the crèche to speak to Nan in person and hold Julia in her arms for a few minutes. But such behaviour would lead to questions, and at the moment she had no answers. She pressed the memory button again.

'Nan, it's Katy. Could you take Julia home tonight? The new boss wants to talk about my pet project, and if I want it brought up in the ward meeting tomorrow, I'll have to stay and explain it to him.'

Nan's reply was immediate.

'I'd love to have her. You've no idea how I've missed her visits while you were both away, and my kids have been nagging me to have her over as soon as you returned.'

Katy relaxed. Nan's enthusiasm was genuine, and Julia returned her honorary aunt's affection—so much so she kept a toothbrush, pyjamas and spare clothes at Nan's house.

'I'll come down and see her before you go,' Katy promised, then hung up, her fingers tingling with apprehension now the decision was made.

If she had any sense at all she'd have told Jake it was impossible, but she hated telling lies—and to tell the truth would be unthinkable.

She turned back to the messages on her desk and worked through until four. Jake hadn't returned, and Katy assumed he was seeing his afternoon patients. She slipped out of the office and went down to say goodbye to Julia, then returned via the ward to check on the new Vietnamese patient.

Mr Nguyen must have spread the news, for two elderly women were entering the room as she approached. They carried baskets and cloth-covered parcels so she turned away, not wanting to interrupt when the patient had visitors.

Back in her office, she found a copy of the 'New Unit' file and began to check through it, marking sections Jake might query and mentally preparing her argument in support. She was engrossed in an article she'd included about the use of steam for purification when the fire alarm sounded.

Her first reaction was to race down the fire stairs and check on Julia, but she knew she must see to her own section first. As she hurried into the foyer she recognised the signal as a localised alarm, then the noise stopped.

'That's it?'

She turned to see Jake emerging from the elevator.

'Repeated long blasts signal a major emergency,' she explained. 'That long-short noise indicates the extinguishers have come into operation in one section of the building. When the alarm stops, you know the fire is out.'

As she spoke she heard a commotion in the corridor beyond the foyer, and saw the visiting Vietnamese women emerging from Mrs Nguyen's room.

They were wet!

'Oh, no!' she groaned. 'Not today!'

Leaving Jake in the foyer, she raced towards them, propelling herself past their chattering laments and into the suite.

The new mother was sitting on a chair, her baby held tightly in her arms. A nurse was stripping off the wet bedclothes and a wardsman was mopping the floor. For a moment she thought the woman was as wet as her visitors, then she realised they were tears on her cheeks. Beside her, Mr Nguyen was re-rolling his umbrella, and Katy chuckled as she visualised him calmly using it to protect his wife and child from the downpour while pandemonium erupted among the staff and visitors.

Jake arrived with Helen close behind him.

'What's going on?' he demanded, and Katy pointed towards the small brass urn almost under the bed—now full of sooty water.

'My wife's friend brought it in,' Mr Nguyen explained. 'She believes in the old ways—in the "roasting" after birth. She brought only a small amount of charcoal but it must have smoked too much. We meant no harm...'

He spread his hands and frowned ferociously, as if concerned the debacle might cause his wife's expulsion from the hospital.

Helen looked at Katy and sighed. It had happened once before, and the sprinklers had worked efficiently both times, but it was the worst possible recommendation for the new unit.

'Roasting?' Jake repeated in a weak voice.

'I'll explain later,' Katy told him. A wardsman wheeled in a dry bed, and while Helen held the baby Katy helped a nurse transfer the woman to it.

'We'll take the baby down to the nursery,' Helen told the father. 'He seems dry enough but we'd better check him out. Would you please tell your wife we'll have to move her into the ward while we clean up in here.'

As the young man turned to his wife to explain what was going on Helen murmured to Katy, 'At least there the passing staff can keep an eye on things.'

Katy listened to the flow of foreign words and thought their patient seemed more comforted than upset. Maybe the 'roasting' had been too much for her as well!

'Come along, Miss Turner,' Jake said, tapping her on the shoulder as she bent to admire the baby once again. 'You've got some extra talking to do!'

She followed him back to their office where he pushed the 'New Unit' file to one side and turned his chair so he could look directly at her.

'Now, as you're the local expert on ethnic culture, perhaps you can explain how a visitor damn near set fire to the hospital.'

Katy eyed him warily, unable to judge if he was angry or amused.

'The hospital was never in any danger.' She plunged into her defence with a stout heart. 'The fire alarms are so sensitive even burning toast will set them off.'

'So, do we remove all the fire sensors in the maternity ward when Asian patients are in residence?'

The question was asked with such silky restraint it prodded anger into life.

'Don't be ridiculous!' She flung out her arms in exasperation, knocking over her prized brass pelvis. 'The whole point of the new unit is not a place so much as an approach. I've already said that the hospital needs to set up antenatal clinics for these women which will include group discussions on childbirth and confinement, but it's a two-way street, Jake. We can listen to these women and try to understand what they want, but it also gives us the opportunity to explain the way the hospital works—including the fact that we have fire sensors in all rooms, and that water sprays from the ceilings if smoke is detected.'

He reached out and picked up the fallen ornament, running his fingers over the smooth metal.

'Okay, I take that point. Now perhaps we could go back to today's little disaster and the term they used. "Roasting", wasn't it?'

Katy felt a surge of hope.

'You've got to understand that a great deal of Asian medicine is based on what they call "humours",' she began.

'The concepts of hot and cold, of yin and yang.' He nodded as if he'd heard or read of this.

'That's right,' Katy agreed. 'If you can go along with the concept of hot and cold, then you'll understand when I say most Asian women believe the loss of blood during childbirth leaves them cold. In almost all of their cultures there are provisions for confinement that concentrate on keeping the body warm.'

'Which is why, on a warm day, that woman was rugged up like a football spectator outside on a winter afternoon.'

Katy grinned at him.

'Dreadful, isn't it?' she agreed. 'But that's to our way of thinking. And that's why her friend brought in the little fire-pot. Vietnamese women, in particular, believe the body benefits by lying over a fire. To them, it not only replaces lost heat but it helps dry up the lochia and shrink the woman's tissues back into place. In parts of China it's called "lying in the fire". Some cultures observe the ritual for three days, while others believe you must keep it up for the whole month.'

'Doing the month,' he murmured, and she remembered he had asked about it earlier.

She was wondering where she could begin her next explanation when his pager buzzed and he turned away to press a number on his phone.

He was as quick on the uptake as he'd always been, she realised, listening as he switched from one conversation to the next. She felt pleased the head injury he'd received in the accident hadn't left any lasting legacy, then chided herself for caring what had happened to him.

Professional efficiency, Katy! she reminded herself, and turned the thought to her own advantage.

Surely his intellectual ability should help him grasp the importance of establishing the new unit—although it was a leap of faith to hope he'd understand it all in twenty-four hours. She had been studying the language, customs and culture of these women for two years and still understood so little. How could she explain to someone who had no prior knowledge, had done no background reading on the subject?

'I'll have to leave it till later,' he murmured, slipping his hand over the mouthpiece on the phone while he spoke to her.

She nodded her agreement and turned her attention back to the work that was still clogging the surface of her desk.

Fire report first, she reminded herself, and got up to find the correct form in the filing cabinet. Helen would fill in a similar form, as would the fire officer. Katy smiled to herself. One of her recurring nightmares was of Lake Shore North disappearing under a snowstorm of official forms and duplicated paperwork.

'I'm going down to Cas; there's a pregnant woman who's been involved in a minor traffic accident and the resident on duty is concerned about her. If I don't get back before you're ready to leave, I'll see you up-stairs—top floor, first door on the left.'

He touched her shoulder as he walked past and she felt her skin burn where his fingers had brushed it.

You can't still love him, she told herself, despair weighing down her heart. He treated you like some worn-out belonging, to be thrust aside as soon as he was finished with it. Where's your pride, girl? Or your instinct for self-preservation?

By six o'clock she knew she could put off their next meeting no longer. She'd been on the phone to Admin over a hitch in a ward orderly's holiday pay when Jake had come back into the office, picked up the file, and pointed his finger upwards to indicate he was on his way to his temporary abode.

More reluctant than she'd ever felt, she hesitated a moment longer, then rang Nan and spoke to Julia, need-ing to shore up her defences against Jake Cartwright.

'Been busy?' he asked when she finally pushed open the first door on the left and stepped tentatively into a pleasantly furnished sitting room.

'Always.' She crossed to the window, diverted and delighted by the spectacular view. 'I had no idea the hospital had accommodation up here.'

The wind had dropped and the sun was setting. The flaring colours in the western sky had turned the lake to a gleaming sheet of red, gold, pink and amber.

'Remember rowing into the sunset, Katy?' he asked, and she felt her shoulders curl instinctively forward, as if to protect the soft, vulnerable parts of her body. She'd been thinking of that evening herself, of the soft splash of sound as they'd rowed, and the way the colour had seemed to flow below the surface, following the cuts they'd made as they dug the oars into the water.

'It was like a different world—the hot colours—fire and blood—claimed as ours—as symbols of our passion and our work.'

His voice was husky, tempting her to fall in with this nostalgic journey to the past. Her stomach tightened.

It was one thing to take that walk alone—to remember the good times occasionally. But to do it with Jake? To indulge in an orgy of 'remembers' with him? No way!

'They don't last long, the colours of sunset,' she pointed out, seeing the rose give way to violet, the orange to a burst of red before fading to darkness. Nor does love, she could have added, but instead she said, 'I think I prefer the lake in daytime.' Her voice was far calmer than her intestines. 'Cool colours—blue and green, muted greys and wind-flecked white. That's when the lake looks most beautiful to me.'

'What about silvered by the moonlight, Katy?' he tempted, but she refused to play the game. She closed her eyes against this next intruding memory, then opened them to pick out landmarks in the business district of the city at the southern end of the lake.

'That new tall building is an insurance office,' she said, to make sure he'd got the message that 'let's remember' wouldn't work with her, although her skin and bones belied this thought.

He muttered a reply, but she refused to speculate what it might have been. Instead, she concentrated on standing upright, keeping calm and studying the city lights, which seemed brighter now the sun had gone.

Somewhere beyond the stacked lights of the office towers was Lake Shore General, where she had trained

and Jake had worked, and beyond that again the arid
suburb where she'd grown up—the rented house sur-
rounded by a straggle of grass she'd once tried to turn
into a lawn.

'Do you ever see your father?'

Damn the man. He'd followed her thoughts as easily
as if she'd drawn a map.

'No,' she said. 'I tried to once, but he made it very
clear he still considers me the cause of all the misery in
his life.'

'Still hasn't occurred to him he had something to do
with your mother becoming pregnant?'

The words were spoken lightly, but Katy could remember Jake's disbelief when she'd told him of the life
she'd lived, caught between two bitter, warring, unfor-
giving parents and held responsible for their misery.

'It doesn't bother me,' she told him.

'Much!' he teased, and she knew he was probably
right. She might have put her childhood behind her, but
the experiences of her early years intruded into the
choices she'd made as an adult. Especially in regard to
bringing Julia up in a single-parent household. Two loving parents might be better than one, but without love...

She shrugged off his intimated doubt.

'I rarely think about it,' she told him—and that was
the truth. She rarely thought of anything prior to Jake's
advent into her life, and she'd already moved out of that
depressing suburb by the time she met him, moving
north towards the lake—like going up a kind of domi-
ciliary ladder.

'I live down there now,' she said, and peered downward and to the right. She could almost see the semi-
detached cottage where she and Julia lived. It was further
north again. Not that upward social mobility had per-

suaded her to buy where she had; she'd chosen the area because it was within walking distance of the hospital and the lake. Paying for it was difficult, but it was the perfect house for her and Julia.

'Can you see your house?' he asked, moving closer.

She stepped casually away from him, pretending she was moving to have a better view. Actually, she'd have needed to be an ostrich to see her place from here, but it seemed a reasonable excuse to edge away.

'No, but I know it's down there.'

She saw him smile and knew he was remembering how possessive she'd always been over having her own living space.

'Shift in with me,' he'd said so often in the past. 'This place of yours is smaller than my bathroom.'

'But it's mine,' she'd argued fiercely. 'My home!'

More of a home than the houses she'd lived in as a child was what she'd meant. And, back then, he'd come to understand.

She turned from the window and walked across to sit in one of the easy chairs.

'Well, tell me what you think of my temporary abode?' Jake waved his hand around his domain. 'They keep the suites for visiting bigwigs—or temporary employees like me.'

He must have walked up behind her while she was reliving flashes of her life, for his words rustled over her shoulder and her skin tingled again with its acute awareness of his presence. But he'd also switched the conversational tone back to purely business, and for that she was grateful.

'Must save Old Forbes a fortune in hotel accommodation,' she replied as lightly as she could manage, shrugging off the potency of his body's closeness.

'Mr Forbes not your favourite administrator?' Jake teased, and she smiled at the question.

'Actually, I quite enjoy our battles, and I think he feels the same way. If the administration in a hospital this size isn't tight, then money that could be providing better patient service is frittered away. And of course there are the factional fights as well!'

She could be as businesslike as he.

'It's the same as any huge organisation,' she explained. 'Every department wants a bigger slice of the pie. Neurology has a top-rate director's assistant. It's a man, and, though I hate to admit it, he's the best in the hospital at wheedling money out of—'

'Old Forbes?' Jake interrupted, and Katy realised she'd been talking too much—probably to hide her nervousness. Surely he couldn't still affect her like this?

Couldn't he what!

'Did you have time to read the file?' she asked abruptly.

He pointed to the pile of papers on a small table beside one of the room's three easy chairs.

'I've read the summary of what you want, but haven't had time to read all the supporting documents. What if we order dinner, then go through the summary and you can tell me why each point is important? That way, if I have to discuss it before I finish the documentation, I'll have some basis for argument.'

He sounded so composed Katy wondered if she'd imagined a different texture in their conversation earlier—a tension fired by one round of 'do you remember?'.

Or was she keyed up because of that unexpected kiss this morning?

Or some hidden hope still lingering in her wishful, foolish heart?

CHAPTER FOUR

THE meal arrived as Katy was explaining the concept of 'hot' and 'cold' foods.

'So "hot" doesn't mean cooked or heated in this context; it means spicy or salty.' Jake poked at his steak as he spoke and grimaced slightly.

'That's right,' Katy agreed, smiling at the expression on his face. 'And in the context of the canteen kitchen, "medium rare" means however it comes off the griller. That's why I always have the sausages. There's not much can go wrong with sausages.'

She thought she'd raise a smile, but he studied her across the table, then frowned instead.

'I should have taken you out for dinner,' he said, surprising her with the vehemence in the words.

'Hey, it's a business meal, that's all.' She spoke casually, to hide the flutter of unacceptable excitement in her chest. 'It's more important to get through the work than to have a gourmet dinner.'

She tackled the sausages and they ate in silence for a while.

'I'm not so sure,' he said grouchily, still prodding at the steak

'I am,' Katy told him firmly, and continued with her explanations. He didn't interrupt, eating absentmindedly while she talked about the adjustments Lake Shore North had already made.

'The food business has been sorted out. We have so many Asian patients in other parts of the hospital it made sense to employ some Asian cooks. We have menus printed in Chinese and Vietnamese and patients can make their own choices.'

Katy cut into a sausage. This eating with Jake had a peculiar intimacy, and she had to struggle to keep her mind on the discussion.

'Menus are easier to sort out than fires under the beds,' he suggested.

'Why?' she demanded, pushing her fork into the cheesy top of the scalloped potatoes. 'I realise we can't have actual fires, but there are air-conditioning controls in all the rooms and all wards. It's impossible to heat a particular room when the rest of the building is being cooled, but the air-conditioning could be turned right down in the new unit. If we can provide the proper counselling during pregnancy, and make certain the staff allow the women to wear their layers of clothing, there'd be no need for fires.'

Her meal was plain but good, and she paused to take another mouthful.

'That's a point.' He finished his steak and pushed his plate away. 'And an argument in favour of keeping these women together in one ward. What else?'

'Showers!' Katy groaned as she remembered some of the battles she'd fought over the showers.

'Showers?' Jake echoed.

She nodded and grinned, her dinner forgotten.

'You've worked in enough hospitals to know how important the daily routines are to nursing staff—particularly the cleanliness routine. Can you imagine the nurses' horror when I suggested something as depraved as not forcing these patients to shower?'

Jake chuckled at her expression of mock-horror. 'Okay, do tell!'

'It's the hot-cold thing again—or it may be to do with body humours—but these women believe water—and especially cold water—is to be avoided during the period after the baby's birth. They think showering or bathing too soon after childbirth will bring on arthritic pains in later life, while hair-washing will lead to hair loss. In some cultures the restriction on bathing and hair-washing only lasts a few days, but in others it is for the whole month. The women keep themselves clean by sitting in steam and wiping the perspiration from their bodies. They use aromatic herbs and spices which they believe helps this purification process, but they don't leap out of bed and have a shower every morning.'

'That must horrify the nurses!'

'And most other patients,' Katy pointed out. 'Some of the women leave hospital days before they should be discharged because they are either intimidated into showering or because the other patients make them feel dirty. It's a difficult position for staff and patients, but, again, if these women could use a particular ward we could set up a portable sauna or steam bath for them.'

Jake shook his head, as if bemused by the extent of her knowledge.

'I can't believe you've gone into it all so thoroughly. What started you on it?'

'When—' She stopped abruptly, aware she'd almost said, When Julia was born. 'I have a Chinese friend who taught me the language. We used to sit and talk in a mixture of English and Chinese, mostly about the hospital and her experiences having her first baby in Malaysia and her second baby here. I was interested in the differences—'

'And began to study them? You've done an enormous amount of work to prepare this file.'

He spoke admiringly but she couldn't take the praise.

'Most of it was organising other people to write papers,' she told him. 'For example, one of the papers is by a woman doctor. She belongs to the Hmong people, a race of Chinese origin spread throughout South-East Asia.'

'She was a doctor in this hospital?' Jake asked, and Katy shook her head.

'I met her when she came to Lake Shore North to have her first baby. She had been educated here, and with her medical training she didn't believe in the old ways. Naturally she didn't "do the month", didn't stay quietly at home with her baby as custom dictates, or avoid water, or keep warm. The baby slept in its own room instead of with her, and she actually hired a nanny and returned to work part-time—'

'And her hair fell out?'

It was a gentle tease, not meant to scoff at her explanation, and she smiled at him.

'No, but she wasn't well. Nothing specific—coughs and colds, aches and pains, general debility—'

'Which could be the natural result of trying to handle a new baby and a career at the same time,' Jake broke in.

'Exactly,' Katy pointed out. 'Most customs develop from actual experience. These ancient rules didn't come about by accident. By insisting the woman takes it easy for a month, for whatever reason, it gives her time to recover her strength, establish the baby on the breast and get used to having this little human being dependent on her. Even the bathing restrictions possibly stemmed from a time when the only water in the village could have been contaminated. By avoiding water for a month, the

woman lessened the risk of infection for either herself
or the baby.'

'So what happened to your friend?'

He was leaning forward now, his elbows on the table
and his chin propped in his hands. She could see his
fingers—long and slim, laced together—and if she lifted
her gaze just a little higher she'd meet his eyes.

She looked towards the window instead, afraid of a
growing warmth in the room that had nothing to do with
the temperature or the discussion.

'She had another child almost immediately, but this
time she ''did the month''.' She turned back to him and,
seeing the glint of laughter in his eyes, she smiled.

'No, she didn't roast herself,' she told him, 'but she
did stay at home, she did keep warm and she did eat the
recommended foods. She's a woman brought up and
educated in our Western system, yet she admitted to me
that she hoped by doing it properly the second time she
might undo any long-term harmful effects caused by her
first confinement.'

He shook his head—disbelieving of the theory yet accepting these concepts he didn't fully understand.

'I'll fight for your unit, Katy,' he said, in such a gentle
voice she was suddenly afraid.

'Thanks!' she muttered, rising abruptly to her feet.
'Well, I'll get going now and leave you to read through
the rest of the stuff.'

She grabbed her handbag from the coffee table and
headed towards the door.

'I'll see you tomorrow!'

'Hey, what's the rush? I was going to offer you coffee—I have a very fancy machine supplied in what they
call the ''kitchenette''.'

'I'd better go,' she said, barely hesitating in her forward rush.

'Then I'll see you to your car,' he protested, and she knew she must be imagining the disappointment in his voice.

'I don't have a car—I w-walk!' she stuttered. He was far too close, the room too small—he was taking all her air again!

'Then I'll walk with you,' he said firmly, and his hand closed around her arm as he ushered her towards the door.

They rode down in the lift in silence, but when they crossed the main entrance lobby on the ground floor Katy knew she had to break it. It was constricting her, drawing her closer to Jake, making her feel too familiarly comfortable with him.

As they stepped out through the front door an ambulance siren ripped through the night. Although it was a common enough sound around her work-place, she never heard one without remembering their background chorus, screaming in and out of the A and E entrance, the night she had sat with Jake while they'd fought to stabilise him.

'Do you remember much about being brought here after the accident?' She asked the question unthinkingly —a kind of word-association response. And then wished she hadn't!

'Enough of it, Katy,' he said gravely.

He took her arm again as they crossed the road and made their way towards the path that led through the park to the lake's edge. It was the path she took when walking to and from work, but he didn't know that. He was steering her that way because they'd walked there in the past and because he had more to say to her than, 'Enough of it, Katy'.

Something in his voice, or the tension straining from his body, gave her the warning, but she had no idea how she might deflect him from talking of that time. They reached the lake and he drew her towards a seat that faced the moon-silvered waters.

'You were right, all those years ago, when you accused me of being wild and reckless—of always having to go that one step too far, having to prove something to myself,' he began quietly. 'The wild and reckless bit was tamed, somewhat, but for the rest...'

Pain surfed along her nerves. It was the daredevil in Jake which had appealed to her, for she had felt the same rash determination. Only in her case it was directed towards achievement in her work—an achievement that had come too easily to Jake to provide the challenges he needed.

'I might have criticised you for it, but it was probably the one quality that saved your life,' she argued, remembering his early unconscious state, the severity of his blood loss, kidney damage—the list had gone on and on. 'Sheer bloody-mindedness would have goaded you to prove all the medical experts wrong.'

He chuckled at her words.

'You may be right,' he agreed. 'Although at times I wondered if the fight was worth it.'

'Of course it was!' She leapt to reassure him, for a world without Jake—even a Jake who no longer loved her—would be inconceivable.

He didn't seem to hear her. His eyes remained focused on the water and he shifted, a little uneasily, on the hard wooden seat. She remembered that suggestion of a hesitation in his stride and wondered if his hip still pained him.

'Of course it was!' he echoed, breaking into her thoughts of his mangled hip. 'But it took a long time and then I had to find a job—I hadn't completed my two years' residency, so the powers-that-be decreed I should start the second year again. By the time I finished I knew I wanted to specialise in Obstetrics and Gynaecology. That took another two years, and then I had a stint overseas for twelve months.'

The night wrapped them in a velvety cloak of grey. Along the path, puddles of yellow light lay like patterns in the soft material. The water lapped against the shore, caressing the shelving sand. Katy absorbed the sights and sounds unconsciously, taking in the water's voice as a kind of counterpoint to Jake's story and listening to it in the silences that fell between his words.

'I came back to a position at a hospital in Perth and did well there. I was doing some teaching, taking students for seminars, becoming involved with an IVF programme...'

Somewhere in the park a curlew cried, its mournful note echoing a kind of loneliness she sensed in Jake's words. She steeled her heart against a stabbing wedge of pity.

Feel sorry for Jake Cartwright?

Never!

'Well, what happened next?' she asked briskly, as if his recitation had been simply a statement of facts to her. 'Did Perth disappoint you? Was the triumphal return to the old home town not quite what the prodigal expected?'

She stood up so he wouldn't sense her agitation and began to walk slowly down the path. For some reason she couldn't bear to think of her carefree, laughing Jake unhappy. He caught up with her and walked beside her, not touching her, until they reached the place where two swans slept, like folded white towels left by the edge of the lake.

If he mentions the swans I'll scream, Katy decided. Enough is enough with this delving into the past!

But he didn't mention the swans.

'Nothing was as I expected, Katy,' he said quietly. 'Or everything and nothing.'

He paused, but she was beyond conversation. The shock of seeing him again, and the continued pressure of his presence throughout the day, had left her feeling quite exhausted. She needed to regroup—to regather the energy she needed to deal with another thirty-nine days of Jake.

She strode ahead, taking the path that cut back towards the end of her street. It led through an avenue of spreading poincianas, their canopies knitted together to blot out the night sky.

'I hope you don't walk home this way after dark,' he said, and his voice had a gravelly sound which scraped along her nerves.

'I rarely walk home after dark,' she said, deliberately distancing himself from his concern. When they regained the road she pointed across it. 'My place is there—the second house along that street. I'll be quite all right from here.'

Her voice was tight with the strain of speaking normally. She wanted to run away, or shout at him to leave her alone—and she certainly didn't want him intruding into her home, didn't want images of his presence left behind like forgotten socks when he walked out of her life again.

She also couldn't risk his seeing the evidence of Julia's existence—the scattered toys, the doll's house they were building out of Lego blocks.

He must have sensed her reluctance, for he paused, then drew her back into the shadow of the trees and turned her so she faced him. In the dim light his face was unreadable, yet she knew his tension was as great as hers. It crashed against her in the darkness, invisible waves pounding on her skin.

'I rebuilt my life from almost nothing, Katy,' he continued, as if there'd been no pause, no conversational shift. 'Bit by bit I put myself back together again— learning first to stand and then to walk again. I retrained my head to read and absorb what it was reading, to think medically and retain knowledge. I worked hard at it and I succeeded, achieving top marks in my specialty exams. I was invited to join hospital staffs, to teach, to be involved in projects. It became a busy life—frenetic, professionally fulfilling—yet as empty as a school during holiday time. The buildings are still there, but there's a desolation about such places…'

She felt his anguish as a burning in her chest, but she shied away from hearing more. She moved, but his hand tightened on her arm.

'Six months ago I began to wonder if it wasn't what I'd won that was bothering me but what I'd lost.'

He leaned forward and pressed a kiss on her forehead. It was as chaste as a child's shy salute, yet it burnt into Katy's skin like a red-hot cattle brand.

Her heart was beating so erratically she could barely breathe, yet she couldn't contain the anger that fizzed and bubbled in her blood.

'*You* broke off our relationship, Jake!' she retorted scornfully. 'You told me it was over, finished, gone and done for—you told me you'd known that for some time, even before the accident. You refused to see me, you returned my letters unopened, you offered me no apology or explanation, just, "It's over, Katy". And now you've got the hide to breeze back into my life and talk about emptiness.'

She resisted an urge to stamp her foot. Instead, she dragged fresh air into her lungs and continued, 'Well, let me tell you this, Jake Cartwright. I know all about emptiness. In fact, I'm an expert on it. And it won't kill you! You can learn to live with it—you can even learn to hide it from yourself.'

'So you don't feel the same? You've found happiness with someone else?'

His voice seemed to be coming from a long way off, but Katy knew it was the echo of her anger roaring in her ears that distanced it. She considered lying, but truth was too important to her.

'I've found a life I enjoy, work I love and contentment, Jake. I was never the risk-taker you were,' she said. 'And that hasn't changed.'

'So, going out with me again, even on an "old friends" basis, would be a risk?' he challenged, his voice full of teasing laughter, as if all his doubts had suddenly been banished.

She tried to work out what she'd said to change his mood, but couldn't find an answer. The temptation to say yes was so strong she felt her lips moving. Then she remembered Julia.

Seeing Jake again had made her realise just how deeply she still cared for him—and that she always would. She knew exactly what he meant about that sense of emptiness, for there was a part of her which would never be complete without him.

But he had said he loved her once before and turned away from her; there was no guarantee he wouldn't do it again. If she'd had only herself to consider, she'd have walked back into his arms—and probably into his bed—and suffered the consequences later. But there was no way in the world she'd risk that happening to Julia, risk her suffering the devastation of loss which was still so vivid in her own mind.

'It would be a disaster, Jake,' she said firmly. 'Believe me!'

'Perhaps,' he said, 'but couldn't we at least find out.'

'Find out I still love you, but that you don't love me?' she demanded, irony icing her voice. 'That would be fun! However, perhaps this time I'll decline. I'll stick to poking my fingers in electric light sockets for my thrills.'

'I had my reasons, Katy,' he said, so quietly she almost missed the words. Or wished she had!

'I've got to go,' she said, ignoring the implied explanation she doubted he was going to give.

He nodded then, and stepped out of the shadows.

'I'll watch you home from here.' He seemed to sense her reluctance to let him encroach any further into her life. 'See you tomorrow.'

And now she, who'd been desperate to get away, found it difficult to move, so he had to half turn her and press his hand against her shoulder when the road was clear and she could safely cross.

She let the touch propel her forward, taking one step at a time with a mechanical efficiency—increasing the physical distance between herself and her Nemesis, but unable to shut out his emotional presence.

There'd been confusion and uncertainty lurking behind his strange confession, and those two characteristics were so foreign to the Jake she'd known it hurt her to think about them.

And why did it hurt her? The question popped into her head as she unlocked her front door.

She slipped into the sanctuary of her home but did not turn on a light. Instead, she leaned against the door, trying to shut out both the present and the past.

Because she still loved him!

Her heart hammered out the answer, then quivered with fear. At least, she hoped it was fear!

She called in at the crèche to see Julia before work, spending half an hour with her daughter before making her way reluctantly upstairs. If the new unit project was approved, she would have an enormous amount of work to do organising it and setting up the programmes she wanted put in place. The two months would be over before she caught breath.

She sighed deeply, only realising it had also been noisy when her fellow passengers in the elevator swivelled their heads to stare at her. The doors opened on Four and she hurried out. The new unit had assumed even more importance now. It would give her a focus, divert her thoughts away from Jake and keep her so busy her body would be too tired to be seduced by his presence.

Her reluctance to face him became impatience. If he was in the office, she'd stress the importance of the project once again.

'We've managed to group five Asian patients together in 'C',' Rosa Williams, the sister in charge of Ward 'C' announced as she caught Katy's arm and halted her headlong rush along the corridor. She led Katy towards the ward.

'They're a bit of a mix—one Cambodian, your Vietnamese friend, a young woman who came over as a student from Malaysia, another Vietnamese woman who's just had her third baby here and an older Chinese woman from Hong Kong.'

Katy smiled as she imagined the diversity of culture and custom in the small group. She followed Rosa into the ward and spoke to the patients, pleased to see that the grouping appeared to be working. All the women were either cradling their babies or had them sleeping in cribs beside them. Not wanting to be separated from their child was another characteristic of the Asian mother.

She greeted them in Chinese and heard the shy replies in a mixture of languages, then the chatter continued. Katy was delighted by the interaction between the women. Although she had no doubt the Chinese woman spoke perfect English, and was obviously wealthy, she was deferring to the older Vietnamese mother, calling her 'younger aunt' as a sign of respect for her experience.

'My mother has been writing to tell me things I should do after the baby is born,' she told Katy, 'but I did not understand why she was so insistent until Auntie explained. What do you think?'

Katy turned the question over to Rosa, but before she could reply a male voice answered.

'I think you must do whatever makes you comfortable.'

Katy knew he was drawing closer, awareness plucking at her skin. She was wrong! No matter how much work she had to do—no matter how busy she kept herself—the two months *wouldn't* be over before she caught her breath. In fact, the way she was reacting to his reappear-

ance in her life, she doubted she'd ever breathe normally
again.

'We Western doctors are using more and more tech-
niques from other cultures, particularly ancient Chinese
teachings,' Jake continued. 'On a recent visit to Beijing,
I saw a Caesarean operation performed on a patient an-
aesthetised by acupuncture. I'm not saying I'd offer that
option to all my patients, but we must work towards
providing what is best for each individual.'

The woman from Hong Kong smiled openly at him,
but the other women rearranged their bedclothes and
lowered their eyes demurely.

It might be their custom, Katy thought, but it was also
very effective flirting in a way. Even she could see the
appeal of this bashfulness—and she wasn't a male!

'This is Dr Cartwright.'

Rosa introduced Jake and prepared to lead him around
the ward. Katy ducked away, pleased the office would
be empty and she could restore order to her too-
responsive body before he returned.

Which was five minutes before the ward meeting was
to begin!

Perhaps he was avoiding her as assiduously as she
would like to avoid him. He breezed into the room with
a bright good morning, and proceeded to drag his chair
across towards the little coffee table.

'So, Katy.' She turned as he dropped a pile of files
onto the table. He looked up and smiled at her, and she
knew it was probably just a 'friendly co-worker' kind of
smile. It was her reaction to it that was the problem.
'You seem to have the ward staff convinced the new
unit is a good idea. What's the procedure if this meeting
formally endorses it?'

Echoes of the previous night's strange conversation

blotted out her mind for a moment, so when he walked back towards her, she stiffened warily.

'It's up to you to convince the people up top,' she told him. He moved closer, increasing the tension in her body until she jerked away when he touched her arm.

'I need your chair,' he said mildly, but his eyes were laughing down at her as if he knew exactly why she'd reacted as she had.

Hot with embarrassment, she stood up and moved aside, trying to steady the wild beating of her heart.

'Still prefer power points?' he murmured softly, then he stooped and picked up her chair, carrying it across the room to add it to the informal grouping.

She ignored the jibe, staring out of the window to a view hazed by her inward-looking eyes. He was doing this deliberately, she realised. Taunting her with words and touches—as if he needed to prove his power over her.

But why? Was it really to fill the emptiness he claimed he felt—and, if so, for how long would he want her this time? Was it one more challenge for the man who loved a challenge? Or did he simply want to prove the old sex-appeal still worked? Would winning her back—against whatever odds he might perceive—overcome some lingering uncertainty the accident had left in his psyche?

She shook her head, annoyed with her attempts to analyse the man when she should be ignoring him. And even more disturbed by the tiny pinprick light of hope which kept flashing in the darkness of her soul.

What if—?

She slammed the thought away. Surely she'd learnt her lesson where Jake was concerned! She was damned if she'd be used as part of his healing process. And there was Julia, remember...

'So I take it to the top?'

She spun around, frowning as she tried to remember what they'd been talking about—before power points!

'Do you think I'm the man for the job?' he asked. 'Do you think my charm will win the day?'

She knew he was supposedly discussing approval for the new unit, but his intonation underlined another meaning in the words, and the half-smile twitching at his lips sent her heart skittering into the uneven rhythm of a syncopated jazz phrase.

CHAPTER FIVE

KATY was saved from answering by a quiet tap on the door. It opened to admit Helen and Rosa, followed by Ron Spencer and a young woman intern who was doing her O and G term.

'This the lot?' Jake asked.

'Jenny Parish, or someone else from Ward 'A', is still to come,' Helen replied, and then turned as Jenny entered the room.

'I'll get another chair,' Ron offered. 'Seems everyone's turned up to give the new boss the once-over.'

'New temporary boss,' Katy corrected under her breath.

She knew Jake heard the remark, for he winked at her, then, when Ron returned, he waved his hand towards her.

'Katy tells me she could run this office without me, so perhaps I should let her handle the meeting.'

She scowled at him, but produced her agenda and flipped quickly through the early items which were general issues, like rearrangement of schedules with Ward 'A' closed and procedures for dealing with the extra patients in 'B' and 'C'.

When they reached the final item, she asked if anyone had other business to bring up before they discussed the new unit.

'The birthing suites are so popular, I wondered if we might be able to squeeze another one into Ward 'A' if the new unit is established,' Jenny suggested.

Katy watched the pretty nursing sister turn the full force of her charm on Jake and felt a tiny worm of jealousy squirm in her stomach. But Jenny was right. The suites were large rooms furnished to look like fashionable bedrooms. All the paraphernalia of childbirth was hidden away in cupboards behind polished timber doors. The suites were big enough to allow a number of friends or family members to be present at the birth and gave the patient room to move around in the privacy of the suite.

Jenny explained this to Jake and then continued, 'The patient surveys for the last twelve months show six as the maximum number of Asian mothers we've had at one time. Even allowing for an increase once word gets around that we're making a special effort for these women, an eight-bed unit will probably suffice.'

Katy sat quietly. She couldn't argue with that prediction, but she did wonder why Jenny had to swing her shiny dark hair about so much when she was speaking.

'How were the birthing suites set up in the first place?' Jake asked.

'By pinching space from somewhere else,' Helen told him. 'We converted two old labour rooms and closed down one ward to make three suites. It was done about two years ago.'

'Without major upheaval?' Jake asked.

Katy grimaced.

'Hardly! But it's containable,' she said, remembering the chaos while those renovations were completed, 'especially if it's confined to one ward. The worst problem is changing the plumbing for the *en suite* bathrooms. Such refinements hadn't been considered when Lake Shore North was built.'

'Are they necessary in birthing suites?' Jake asked.

'They give the woman an opportunity to take a warm bath or shower during the first stage of labour,' Rosa replied. 'It helps ease the pain of contractions without recourse to drugs. More and more women are seeking drug-free births, so we want to do all we can to encourage them.'

Jake glanced at Ron.

'You have some input?' he asked.

The younger man grinned.

'I know my place in this group,' he said. 'One unacceptable suggestion and they're asking me how many pregnancies I've been through.'

The women chuckled, but Ron was only half-joking. At Lake Shore North there was a move away from specialist attendance at trouble-free births, with the midwives delivering most of the babies.

'However, I have been keeping statistics since I started here six months ago,' he added, 'and, although I wouldn't quote figures outside this room, I'm beginning to believe the literature which claims babies delivered without the use of drugs are more alert and need less intervention after birth.'

The discussion finished with Katy suggesting she contact the hospital architect about plans and Jake agreeing he'd look at the idea when it had been costed.

They moved on to the new unit, and Katy felt a rush of affection for her little team when, one by one, they supported the idea and praised the work she'd done on the proposal.

'I think we should remember that the most important part of the plan is in-service training for the staff,' Jenny reminded them. 'Even if Admin refuse to give the go-ahead, can't we begin to incorporate discussion on the customs of these women into our in-service programme?'

Jake frowned at her.

'That's not already being done throughout the hospital?' he asked, and she shook her head.

'But you said the hospital has a large number of Asian patients and the kitchens are organised. Has no one thought of staff-training?'

'It's not as big an issue for patients in other departments because they're in for medical reasons or surgical procedures. Geriatrics have been trying to get something organised because they see a number of patients approaching death—which, like childbirth, has certain customs attached to it,' Ron Spencer explained. 'The culture clash only occurs when our way of doing things interferes with their traditions.'

'We've all thought of staff-training,' Helen put in, 'but no one person has the knowledge to draw up a staff-training programme incorporating all the countries involved or all the fields of medicine. It's a one-off project which would require someone working full-time for perhaps six months, contacting experts in medicine from the different backgrounds and asking them to contribute. Considering she has a very demanding job, Katy's done wonders with our small section, but she can't be expected to do any more.'

Katy turned to Jake and saw he understood the magnitude of the problem. His eyes were grave as he considered Katy for a moment, then he nodded as if he'd come to a decision he wasn't going to share.

'I'll speak to someone about it,' he said, 'but, in the meantime, circulate the articles Katy's gathered among your staff. The more background knowledge they have, the more tolerant they're likely to be.'

He leaned forward and stacked his folders into a neat pile, indicating the meeting was almost over. He was assuring them he'd seek approval to set up the unit straight away when there was a light tap on the door. Katy went to answer it and found a hospital volunteer standing outside, almost hidden by a huge arrangement of flowers.

'You're Katy Turner, aren't you?' the woman asked, and when Katy, too astonished to speak, nodded, she thrust the arrangement into her arms.

'The delivery man left them at the front desk,' the volunteer explained. 'Must be nice to have someone who loves you that much.'

Katy felt the blood rushing upward to stain her cheeks. Jake used to send her flowers... Surely not!

She backed into the room, wishing she could hide the gift, but the sheer size of the bouquet made that impossible. She sneaked a look at Jake and caught the dark shadow of anger on his face, but then it vanished, replaced by a remote mask.

Jake hadn't sent the flowers!

She dropped them on her desk, too embarrassed to even think of looking for a card.

'That's some floral tribute!' Helen remarked as Katy slunk back to her chair.

'Such lavish attention doesn't look like John's style. Was there a great holiday romance?' Jenny smirked knowingly. She'd gone out with John herself for some time and found his interest in Katy a source of great amusement.

Katy seized the agenda and made some comment about that being all for the meeting. But she was wondering how Jake had reacted to Jenny's words and she could feel the flowers looming behind her like some floral science fiction monster that grew and grew.

'Before we finish,' Jake said quickly, 'I've spoken to the head of the interpreting service and arranged for a second female interpreter—so we can take outpatients from this special group fortnightly. However—'

Whatever he was about to say was swallowed up by the alarm that demanded an immediate response. Katy was the first to the door. She thrust her head into the passageway and saw the blue 'B' flashing on a wall monitor.

'It's your ward, Helen,' she said quietly, and stood aside to let the medical team respond.

As Jenny had surmised, the flowers weren't from John. They were from the support group for the sight-impaired she attended, thanking her for her presidency over the last four years. She'd resigned before her holiday, knowing she'd not have the time required to do the job well if she was getting the new unit under way.

She considered the over-size bouquet and realised Jake would have to continue to assume they were from an admirer—which could work to her advantage! If he thought she had a man in her life, he'd stop the subtle campaign he was waging against her. She stared at the flowers for a minute longer, then carried them out into the passage.

'Here!' she told a passing wardsman. 'If you're not busy, could you take these up to the geriatric ward for me. Tell Sister to spread them around. Most of the elderly patients love flowers.'

The man grinned at her.

'Wrong fellow send them?' he teased, and she found herself blushing—although his guess was as wide of the mark as Jake's had been.

She returned to her desk and typed up the minutes from the meeting, then prepared a title page for the submission to the hospital board. The resolution of the ward meeting was set in block letters in the middle of the page, with the names of those present underneath it. As she typed 'Jake Cartwright' she remembered the first time she'd typed his name.

She'd been working in the office of the public hospital at the far end of the lake. It had been a part-time job which helped pay her living expenses while she studied to be a nurse, and as she'd added the final name—his—to the list of new staff members at Lake Shore General she'd looked up to see a pair of blue eyes twinkling down at her.

'Katy Turner—what a crisp, no-nonsense name!' he'd murmured, reading the name-tag pinned to her white shirt. 'Do you do the guided tours around this place?'

She'd blushed and stammered and known almost instantly that she was in love. It hadn't come on her slowly, as she'd expected love to come—creeping up like fog off the lake's edge. It had slammed against her with the suddenness of an automobile accident, and she'd felt the juddering shock ricochet through her body.

Jake Cartwright!

She studied the name and sighed. She could remember that first meeting so vividly, yet the development of their relationship was hazy. Now, nearly eight years on, it seemed as if they'd been together from that day, yet she knew he'd worked impossible hours and she'd studied when she wasn't either typing in the hospital office or waitressing at night.

Maybe their clashing schedules had made the time they spent together feel more precious, more intense, she decided, unconsciously doodling little daisies around his name. Maybe that was why it seemed, now, as if they had never been apart—back then!

Until after that special Easter break, when they'd both had four days off. They'd camped near the beach at Freshwater Cove, swimming, fishing, walking, sleeping—and making love! The memory was like a precious jewel, tucked away in Katy's mind—not brought out too often in case use might dim its lustre.

They'd come back feeling fit and healthy, ready to tackle whatever the new term had to offer. And with such plans! Jake would finish his residency and she would finish her final year at university, then they'd get married.

She slashed her pen across the daisies. The sense of well-being after the holiday hadn't lasted long. In fact, within a fortnight she'd been feeling tired and sick—her stomach so unsettled she'd bought a pregnancy kit at the chemist and tested herself to make sure that pregnancy wasn't the cause.

Jake's working hours had been even worse than hers, yet his energy had remained undiminished. Her increasingly frequent refusals to join him in some 'fun' had led to a tetchiness developing between them—the first shadows of disharmony in what had been close to perfection.

She sighed and turned back to the computer, tapping out a print command to replace the title page she'd ruined.

The door opened and she looked up to see Jake returning.

'I had Giardia, you know!' she said, and only realised she'd spoken her thoughts aloud when she saw the look of puzzlement on his face.

But now the words were said, she decided to continue. 'Before the accident! When I was sick and you were so convinced I was either faking it or pregnant and neither option pleased you very much.'

She snatched up the newly printed page, slipped it into a plastic sleeve on the front of the file and shoved the lot across onto his desk. Then she remembered the crisis call and she looked at him again.

He was frowning, but not at her, and she recognised the look as one he wore when he was inwardly scanning his phenomenal memory banks for some hidden bit of information. He probably hadn't even heard her defiant outburst.

'What was the emergency?' she asked, her own past misery forgotten as she worried about the cause of Jake's distraction.

'That woman who was involved in an accident yesterday,' he murmured. Then he looked directly at her and his eyes came into focus once again.

'Katy, there's a paper in Holstead's *Obstetric Text* about concealed haemorrhage in abruptio placentae. Could you find it for me while I change the infusion we're giving her?'

He disappeared through the door while Katy moved towards the bookshelves. She knew enough medicine to know how dangerous it could be for both mother and foetus when the placenta shifted from the uterine wall. Usually the first indication was uterine bleeding, followed by painful contractions.

Did 'concealed' mean there were no symptoms to guide the medical staff?

She found the article he wanted and began to read it. Problems with supply of blood to the foetus, elevated intrauterine pressure, blood clotting factors seriously depleted. The condition meant danger for both the mother and the child. Had Jake mentioned the woman's term? Would the baby survive if they had to deliver it?

He came back into the room as she was wondering and took the book from her without a word.

'Ah, I thought so!' he muttered to himself, then left the room again before she had time to speak.

It was late afternoon when he returned, and she noticed that his shirt, in spite of the air-conditioning, was wet with perspiration.

'Is she okay?' Katy asked, and was pleased when he nodded.

'And the baby?'

The question clutched at her heart. Babies had become doubly precious to her since Julia's birth.

'We've got him in a humidicrib,' he said, slumping down into his chair and resting his head in his hands. 'Is there a counsellor with experience in premature births who can speak to the mother when she's feeling up to it?'

'Of course!' Katy assured him. 'Helen will take care of that, and will also contact the association for pre-term infants. They're a local group of parents who've had pre-term babies. They have volunteers available for either discussion or assistance.'

She spoke calmly, but her heart was beating out its own anxiety. 'How premature is he?'

'She thought she was thirty-four weeks, but I'm not so certain. He's less than two thousand grams.'

Julia had been seventeen hundred grams. A tiny scrap of humanity, she had looked more like a skinned rabbit than a human baby. Katy glanced at Jake, wanting his reassurance that this baby would be all right. But no one could predict his future at the moment, although with new developments in humidicribs, especially in the way of providing warmth and oxygen supplementation, this baby would have a far better chance than Julia had had, even five years ago.

'Was he delivered vaginally?' she asked.

He looked up and frowned, as if perturbed by her question.

'Why are you asking that?' His frown deepened.

Katy shrugged, aware she'd crossed some imaginary boundary between administration and medicine. Still, he had asked!

'A Caesar would mean the woman is going to suffer physical discomfort for longer, and is therefore weaker and less able to cope with the stress and grief and uncertainty related to giving birth prematurely,' she said, then she ducked her head and pretended to be busy sorting the pile of papers on her desk.

'Grief?' It was only one word but it demanded an answer.

She looked up slowly.

'When a family has a child with problems—even if they are only temporary problems—there is grief for the child they had imagined—the perfect child they thought they were going to have. It doesn't lessen their love for the real baby, but the grief is still there. For a long time counsellors ignored that part of the equation, but, since associations like the pre-term births organisations have been formed, counsellors are accepting what experienced people are telling them.'

He shook his head and smiled.

'I did know that,' he murmured. 'We medicos aren't quite the dehumanised beings some people would have you believe. What surprises me is the depth of your involvement, Katy. I know you worked hard on the unit proposal, and I can understand your commitment to that, but this is a different field and you're just as passionate.'

She was embarrassed by the praise she heard in his voice, but also aware she'd drifted dangerously close to personal issues which had to be avoided at all costs.

'It's my department,' she said defensively. 'It's natural I should be interested.'

'Hmm!' He studied her for a moment, his eyes scanning her face as if he might read a different answer on her skin.

'Well, for your information, Departmental Assistant, she did deliver vaginally. That was what I wanted to check in Holstead. With a concealed haemorrhage the blood has to go somewhere. Usually it escapes into the uterine tissues, causing the uterus to take on a bluish or purplish colour. This condition will resolve itself spontaneously, but Holstead believes vaginal birth will bring a better long-term resolution to the affected tissues. I thought it was worth trying to induce her before operating. Having made that decision, there was a period of very nervous waiting, but it worked in this case.'

He paused, then looked around the room, another frown beginning to pucker the skin between his eyebrows.

'What happened to your flowers?' he asked abruptly, and this time it was she who raised one eyebrow. It was a trick which had taken her years to perfect, but it was enough to remind Jake that her personal life was no concern of his.

She bent over her papers once again, determined to finish her work in time to visit Ward 'B' and the nursery before she left. But it was a pretence. Jake's presence in the room disrupted her thought processes and made the nerves in her skin twitch with awareness. It was impossible to think she could work with him for another thirty-eight days—no matter how busy she might be.

Impossible!

She sighed and thought of Julia, and the mortgage on the house, and the down-payment she'd made on the new computer. She sighed again.

Even more impossible to leave!

'If you've done sighing, would you mind taking this submission up to the administration office for me? Leave it with your mate Mr Forbes and tell him I'd like him to have a look at it before the department directors' meeting next Monday.'

She looked into blue eyes which were regarding her thoughtfully.

'But you said—' she began.

'That I'd argue the case for you,' he interrupted. He slid his hand across the desk and touched her on the forearm. 'And I will, Katy, I will. I've already spoken to Mr Forbes and told him how I feel, but it's only fair he gets an opportunity to read through the proposal before it's discussed. He'll also circulate copies to other departments.'

'They already have copies,' Katy protested mutinously. 'But giving Mr Forbes one this early will give him time to find objections. He'll come prepared with little lists of why the thing's impossible.'

The blue eyes gleamed with mischief.

'So we'll have to prepare our own lists,' he said firmly. 'We'll have to go through it word by word and anticipate his objections, then arrange our arguments accordingly.'

'But that would mean hours and hours of work. We actually have a department to run here, which usually takes all my working hours plus another ten or twelve each week. We'd never get it done!'

The problem was, she knew he was right. In fact, she couldn't understand why she hadn't thought of it herself. When she'd pushed the crèche past administrative barriers she'd had powerful support, as three department directors had pre-school-aged children and problems with suitable childcare. There'd been no need for an extended campaign.

Another sigh slipped from her lips. She should have been doing that kind of analysis during her holidays instead of lying on the beach.

'I beg your pardon?'

She turned to Jake, aware he'd been talking while she chastised herself.

'I said it wasn't like you to quit so easily. You know better than most how hard you have to fight for what you want.'

He looked into her eyes, challenging her to deny his words and carrying her back with effortless ease to long-forgotten arguments.

'But *I* can afford to pay your board and tuition,' he'd said, trying to persuade her to give up her crazy schedule of work and study. 'At least let me keep you.'

'I won't take your charity!' she'd yelled at him. 'I was managing just fine before you came along. I can make it on my own!'

He'd cursed her stubbornness, yet she'd suspected he'd admired it at the same time.

'Well?' he asked, and she realised she'd missed another bit of the conversation. She had to stop flashing in and out of the past. Apart from weakening her mental armour against this man, it was making logical, work-related thought impossible.

'Well?' she echoed in a puzzled voice, trying to pull herself together.

'I said, if we don't have time during the week, we'll have to get together over the weekend. Would Saturday or Sunday suit you?'

'I can't do that!' she gasped. 'I'm far too busy!'

And her time alone with Julia was too precious to consider giving up!

'You were never afraid of extra work,' he reminded her. 'Social life taking up all your time these days?' He looked swiftly around the room, as if to indicate he was thinking about the missing flowers. 'Did your fanatical work ethic finally break down when you realised what you were missing? Is that why you gave up nursing? Did it all get too difficult after all?'

He sounded angry, but puzzled as well—and just a little as if he might care what had happened to her, and why!

'My personal life is none of your business, Jake Cartwright!' she said with regal disdain, then she spoiled the whole effect by adding, 'And I'm still not afraid of extra work. In fact, I still waitress every Friday and Saturday nights, if you must know, which is why I don't want to spend what little spare time I get working on this stupid project!'

He looked stunned by her outburst, but she was already regretting it. The new unit wasn't a stupid project—in fact it was very important to her that it succeeded.

'I can go through the papers on my own during the week,' she muttered. 'After all, I'm the one who knows how Mr Forbes's mind works. I'll jot down the things I think he'll object to and you can work out how you want to respond.'

'Why?' he demanded, the belligerence in his voice dragging her eyes up from her paperwork to focus, again, on his face.

'Why do it?' she snapped. 'You're the one who suggested it.'

He waved his hand as if to dismiss her words.

'Not that,' he said. 'Why are you still waitressing? Aren't you paid enough? Should we be concentrating on admin assistants' wages rather than a new maternity unit?'

She almost smiled. Jake was like a truffle hound when he perceived or suspected injustice!

'I'm paid well, but...' She shrugged her shoulders. She couldn't explain that talking computers with raised characters on their keyboards cost only a little less than a space shuttle, nor could she admit that the two nights a week when she worked as a waitress had become a substitute social life for her.

'I like waitressing,' she finished. Let him argue with that!

She was saved by his pager, which buzzed as she finished speaking. He dialled the number shown, spoke briefly, then stood up.

'I'll be in Theatre if you need me. Mrs Carstairs has come in. And before you ask, she's Dr Anderson's patient, remember? All I'll be is an extra pair of hands. It's not up to me to decide on delivery methods.'

Katy tried to look offended, but it was hard when her lips wanted to smile.

'Dr Anderson agrees with me about natural birth whenever possible,' she said primly. 'She's been taken to Theatre because there's enough space there for five humidicribs and access to more emergency equipment if it's needed.'

He shook his head, as if again surprised by the extent of her knowledge.

'Sure you don't want to take my place in the action?' he teased, and her heart raced into its rapid mode as she caught the full force of his smile.

'Definitely not!' she told him. 'I like the theory, not the practical side of things these days.' She hesitated, then added, 'Good luck!'

He'd been walking towards the door, but he turned and smiled again.

'Thanks, Katy,' he said softly, then he continued on his way.

She stared at the door panels for a moment, unable to escape memories of how things used to be between them. Then she remembered their strange conversation last night, her anger with him, and four words he'd said. ''I had my reasons.''

What had he meant?

She shook her head to rid it of such distraction and phoned through to the chief security officer to warn him that their action plan for the arrival of the expected Carstairs quintuplets should begin. The problem of keeping unwanted visitors off the fourth floor would fall to the security staff, but Katy knew any major disaster— like a photographer flashing his camera in the wards or corridors—would upset patients and staff and undoubtedly rebound onto her.

Bill Head assured her he had it all under control and she hung up and dialled Sue Gates in the nursery.

'I'll ring around for extra staff—is there anyone in particular you want?'

'Thanks, Katy, I was about to call you,' Sue replied. 'Two of the nurses on duty today are willing to take an extra shift tomorrow, but the night sister will need at least two extra helpers—three if you can muster them. Once we know how much work there'll be, I'll juggle the staff to suit. I'd prefer to keep the same rota of staff with the babies, so the little mites aren't constantly re-adjusting to different people.'

'Well, I'll find three for tonight,' Katy promised, pulling a list of casual staff from a drawer in her desk. 'Let me know tomorrow if you need more.'

The hospital's 'casuals' were more like members of a private nursing service, with the hospital contracting them to work in patients' homes, medical centres, or even other hospitals when they weren't required for extra shifts in the wards. Katy's list contained the men and women who specialised in maternity and neonatal nursing. She began her phone calls, knowing whoever she found would need time to make arrangements for childcare or to cancel social engagements before they could report for work.

As she finished the calls she smiled. The first three phone calls had been successful. In fact, the three women she'd contacted had all been delighted at the thought of nursing Lake Shore's expected quintuplets. Knowing Mrs Carstairs's love of publicity, they'd probably all get their photos in the paper!

So cynical, Katy?

She mentally chided herself. The Carstairs family would need all the help it could get in the weeks, months and even years to come. If they could sell their story to the press, good luck to them. But selling to the press brought its own problems, as the media outlet who bought the story would demand exclusive rights. And that would leave all the other news hounds baying at the doors, desperate for an unauthorised picture or story. It made the security angle a nightmare!

But that was a mechanical problem she hoped Security could handle. Less solvable was the future of the babies. Katy worried because she was so aware of the increased risk of abnormalities in multiple births. In fact, considering the statistics, shouldn't there be ethical considerations in using drugs which promoted conception but led to multiple conception? It was something that nagged at her, making her wary about the excitement of the coming event.

She shook her head and decided that the pros and cons of IVF treatments weren't her problem. She'd have enough to worry about with the media circus and staff—things which *were* her concern. Even with extra security staff on the fourth floor, some photographer could find his way into the nursery, anxious to take the first shots of the new arrivals. She'd heard stories where such a thing had happened after the birth of a 'celebrity' baby—only the photographer had photographed the wrong child and the parents had sued the hospital!

She tried to shrug off her feeling of apprehension, telling herself to think positively—there was every chance the whole operation would come off without mishap, that their security precautions would work, and, by far the most important factor, that all five of the babies would pull through the long weeks in the nursery.

CHAPTER SIX

KATY thought of Julia, born at thirty-two weeks, but small for her age, malnourished because Katy's own health had been so poor. For the first forty-eight hours she'd seemed all right, although Katy had thought her lips were cyanosed, and her nostrils flaring too much as the tiny mite gasped for breath. At seventy-two hours the specialist had diagnosed RDS—Respiratory Distress Syndrome. The oxygen saturation in the humidicrib had been increased and Julia had recovered.

It had been months before Katy had realised the full extent of the damage to Julia's eyes. Too late to do anything except be grateful her daughter had survived!

She glanced at her watch. She had twenty minutes before she was due to collect that same daughter from the crèche. She'd take the 'New Unit' file upstairs, then pop into the nursery and see the premature baby before she left.

Mr and Mrs Robinson were sitting by their son's crib, gazing at the baby with wariness, despair and fear intermingling in their eyes.

'Hi, I'm Katy. I work here, but I also had a pre-term baby much the same size as your little lad. She's five now, and has reached all the normal milestones in speech and motor dexterity. In fact, although she's still physically slight for her age, she's ahead of most of her peers in other ways.'

The couple looked up at her, reaching for each other as if they could now fight together for their son.

'It was such a little accident,' the woman said. 'Phil was distracted by a dog. We just bumped the car in front. We were travelling slowly and there was hardly any damage to either car.'

Katy understood the guilt they were both feeling and hastened to reassure them.

'I'm not a medical person, but I know these things can occur spontaneously. The accident might have precipitated it, but it could also have happened without the accident. It's very important not to waste energy apportioning blame but to get on with the positive stuff. Are you hoping to breast feed? Will you express milk so the little fellow can begin feeding on your milk as soon as possible?'

She knew she'd diverted the woman, but Phil was still looking doubtful so she turned her attention to him.

'And will you help with feeding? You can, you know, when they begin to wean him from the crib. At the moment his skin is very fine, and the tiny blood vessels in it are easily damaged, so the less he's handled the better. The staff will show you how to touch him so he knows you're here.'

She gestured towards the crib.

'They curl him in that little nest to help him breathe and keep him warm. Premmie babies haven't had time to put fat down beneath their skin, so they lose heat very rapidly.'

The man was losing his dazed look and Katy felt a sense of relief wash through her. She knew the staff were too busy to spend much time with new parents, and the hospital counsellor was not always available immediately. That was one of the reasons she tried to see the parents herself, before their lack of knowledge and un-easiness built a barrier between them and the child.

'Someone from a pre-term births organisation will probably call in this evening,' she assured them. 'They can help because, like me, they've been through it all and understand how you are feeling.'

The woman smiled at her.

'Thanks for talking to us,' she said softly. 'I think we'll go back to my room now. I feel as if I might be able to sleep for a while.'

Katy watched as her husband helped her to her feet. Would having had someone to lean on have made her time in hospital easier? She'd had Julia in a huge public hospital in a southern city, and the staff had been so busy they'd barely had time to say hello when she'd slipped quietly into the nursery each morning.

Well, it didn't matter now!

She felt her face softening into a smile as she thought of her daughter playing happily downstairs, and hurried from the nursery, anxious now to see her.

They walked home hand in hand, Julia pointing out the flowers on the trees as if she could see them as clearly as Katy could.

'Now we're at the swans,' she announced. 'Are they swimming?'

'They're swimming,' Katy assured her, remembering how Julia had been frightened by the hissing menace of the swans when they'd been nesting. 'And their babies are swimming in line behind them. They're growing some of their white feathers now and don't look nearly as cute.'

'Like the Ugly Duckling in the story,' Julia chortled as they turned into the avenue of poincianas.

Here they walked at the edge of the path so she could

reach out and touch each tree trunk. Katy wondered if she counted her paces between them, for she always knew when to put out her hand so it could slide across the smooth trunk. It was another manifestation of the extra-sensory perception her daughter seemed to have developed to compensate for her loss of sight. It intrigued Katy, and she hoped one day to be able to study the phenomenon in more depth, to work with sight-impaired children and find out if this sensory awareness could be taught like other skills.

There were so many things she wanted to do—one day! Would that day ever come? She doubted it! Her adult life had always been limited by the time she had to give to working to keep herself—and then Julia— alive. Would there ever be a time when she'd be financially secure, so she could stop working for long enough to complete her degree? Or conduct a study into the sensory awareness of sight-impaired children? Or even write a paper on Asian women giving birth in the western world?

Jake had money! The thought insinuated itself into her head.

She wouldn't take it for herself, of course—but for Julia? Her heart beat faster at the implications of the thought, then stilled as she remembered the past.

There was no way she could risk it!

She sighed at the momentary regret.

'You tired, Mum?' Julia asked.

Katy smiled down at her daughter and squeezed her fingers.

'No, love,' she said. 'Just dreaming!'

The jangling summons of the phone woke her from a deep sleep. She glanced blearily at the bedside clock as she lifted the receiver. Nine-thirty! She must have fallen asleep the moment she'd turned the light out ten minutes earlier.

'Hello!'

She tried to make her voice sound alert, annoyed at being caught in bed so early. Julia's fault! Since birth her daughter had been a morning person, and now Katy always woke at five—whether Julia was at home or not.

'It's Jake, Katy. I know I shouldn't be bothering you at home, but I've just got back to the office and needed to talk to someone sane. Fortunately, my predecessor's little book of useful numbers has your home number at the top of the list.'

'Something's wrong?' Her heart was thundering against her chest wall, but she couldn't tell if it was apprehension about work or excitement at hearing Jake's voice on the phone again.

Back when they'd been lovers as well as friends, he'd rung her every evening they'd been apart—rung her to say goodnight and, 'I love you, Katy!'

'Not really!' he said gruffly. 'If you discount Mrs Carstairs's insistence that a film crew be present for the entire delivery, and then Stewart Anderson demanding all but one of them leave and suggesting I help the security men remove them. Then a scuffle with a newspaper photographer in the nursery and one of the security men pulling a gun when the man refused to budge.'

'Oh, Jake! That last bit can't be true,' Katy protested, her voice muffled by the laughter bubbling in her throat. 'The security men don't carry guns, do they?'

She closed her eyes and tried to picture the uniformed men she saw around the hospital each day. But all she saw was Jake's face—older now than her worn images had shown—smiling into the phone.

'Actually, some of them do, I've discovered, but in this case it was a torch. It just looked like a gun,' he told her. 'And the photographer must have thought so, too, because he scarpered.'

'Has it quietened down?'

She heard a shuffling noise, as if he was settling more comfortably into his chair.

'I suppose it's as settled as it can get, with men guarding the main foyer and the fire doors, and all visitors to the fourth floor being screened before they're allowed out of the elevator. But it still won't work, Katy! Someone will eventually arrive to visit one of our other patients and slip away to take whatever snaps they want. Since Mrs Carstairs announced she was having labour pains over talk-back radio this morning, half Australia's media contingent—to say nothing of the usual rush of onlookers and thrill-seekers—have been camped on our doorstep. Most of them arrived before the patient.'

'She announced it on the radio?' Katy echoed. 'I know once a multiple birth had been confirmed she made a great production of the whole pregnancy, much to Dr Anderson's annoyance, but I can't believe she would go that far.'

'Believe it,' Jake told her gloomily. 'She rang the local radio station herself. You must have seen the people gathering outside the hospital when you left. I considered going for a walk—to get some of the air-conditioned air out of my lungs—but when I saw the pack of hounds baying at the main entrance, I headed back up here instead.'

'We go out the back way,' Katy explained. 'I suppose you're lucky you have rooms in the building. The press love photos of the doctors. Poor Dr Anderson will eventually have to run that gauntlet.'

'Not a bit of it,' Jake told her, his voice lightening again. 'He smuggled himself out in an ambulance. Says it happened to him once before. The photographer's flashlight caught him as he was yawning and he ended up with his face splashed across the front page, looking like an incapacitated fish.'

Katy chuckled, remembering the photo Jake described.

'Well?' The single word doused her laughter.

'Well, wh-what?' she stuttered, sensing a shift in the conversation.

'Well, it's your turn to talk, Katy.'

She tried to think of something they could talk about—a conversation which wouldn't stray onto dangerous ground.

'I've started on the list of objections Mr Forbes might have,' she said stiffly, and heard his sigh filter through the airwaves to linger in her ear.

'That's work,' he objected. 'I've had enough of work!'

She knew his voice well enough to know he was smiling as he spoke, although he was pretending petulance. 'Talk to me, Katy, I'm bored' or 'Talk to me, Katy, I'm lonely'. They'd both been common refrains during those other goodnight calls.

The memories were weakening her, and strength was what she needed to deal with Jake.

'We've only work in common,' she told him, hoping she sounded more positive than she felt.

'Not some sharing of the past?' he argued. 'Not memories I haven't forgotten even if you have. What about Freshwater Cove?'

Her stomach shifted uneasily, but she knew she had to make a stand.

'The past is dead and buried, Jake. It died the day you sent me away, but I didn't bury it until my letters were returned.'

There was a silence, then she heard him mutter something indistinguishable.

'I understand how you must feel, how deeply hurt you must have been,' he said more clearly, 'but I don't believe you when you say there's nothing left, Katy. I don't believe it's quite that clear-cut. And I don't believe you believe it either,' he added. 'Goodnight, my love.'

She dropped the phone back into its cradle, blotting the endearment from her mind, turning instead to the puzzle of those indistinct words. She remembered him saying, 'I had my reasons,' yesterday, but she couldn't conceive of a reason with enough validity for him to have cut himself off from her with such deadly precision.

She thought about her own feelings at the time. 'Deeply hurt' didn't begin to cover it! She'd been physically sick, which had added to her devastation, and after the letter telling him she was pregnant had been returned she had told herself she hated him.

But she'd found she couldn't make herself believe it—that she couldn't nurture hate for him at the same time as she was nurturing his baby.

Which didn't mean she'd ever trust him again—whatever he might be trying to make her believe.

She switched out the light and settled down in bed, willing herself to shut out the memories he'd evoked. Willing herself to sleep—not dream of passionate pasts or impossible futures.

The birth of the quintuplets dominated the morning news. Katy turned on the television and saw the pack of photographers camped outside the main entrance to the hospital. Would the security guards have deflected them from the back entrance or would she have to battle through them there as well?

'Can I see the new babies at your hospital, Mum?' Julia asked, tugging at Katy's hand as they left the house.

'They're too little for visitors,' Katy told her, guiding her hopping, skipping daughter safely across the road.

'Someone's waiting under our trees, Mum.'

Julia's remark made Katy pause, clinging to her daughter's hand. They were just inside the boundary of the park, and the avenue of trees was directly ahead of them. In daylight it was a cool green tunnel, and she squinted against the morning glare as she probed the shadows beneath the trees.

He was leaning against the third one along, so still he might have been a part of it. Her lungs felt as if giant hands had squeezed the air from them and she gripped Julia's hand so tightly the little girl cried out.

'Is he a bad man, Mum?' Julia asked, and Katy heard the beginning of panic in her voice. She dropped to her knees and hugged her daughter close.

'No, love, it's a new doctor at the hospital. I didn't see him at first and was startled. How did you know he was there?'

She straightened up, pretending to a normality she didn't feel. She wanted to reassure Julia, not transmit more tension to her.

'He smells like the lemon grass you planted in the back yard.'

Katy sniffed the air. She knew this was another manifestation of Julia's ability to absorb her environment, but she always hoped she might learn to be as proficient with her senses.

There was no trace of lemon grass that she could discern!

'Come on, Mum, we'll be late!'

Julia tugged at her hand and Katy peered warily along the path. Jake hadn't moved—but then, if he'd walked this way to meet up with her, he was probably as shocked as she had been. For the first time since Julia's birth she was glad her daughter was small for her age. At least he wouldn't suspect...

She forced her feet to move, and as she drew closer she even fixed a smile on her lips.

'Good morning, Dr Cartwright,' she said formally. 'This is my daughter, Julia.'

His face looked grey, and she told herself it was the effect of the light beneath the trees. She found she didn't want Jake hurting, no matter what he'd done to her. She turned away, pretending to be looking at the lake, unable to meet whatever emotion might be lurking in his eyes.

Julia reached out and found his hand.

'We're late, Dr Cartwright,' she said, leading them both along the path. 'I told Mum you were under the trees and she thought you might be a bad man.'

Realising she now had two supports, she swung between them while Katy battled the tumult in her body, trying to will herself to behave as if this was a perfectly normal morning. She remembered the major news event with relief!

'How are the new arrivals?' she asked, glancing his way very briefly, then concentrating on the path as if it might have thrown up horrendous obstacles overnight.

'Two are battling—the others should be okay,' Jake replied, and she knew from the strain in his voice that his conversational effort was as forced as her own.

'You've seen the new babies?' Julia asked him,

swinging again so suddenly that Katy snapped at her to stop.

'I have,' Jake replied. 'They are very, very small.'

'I was very small,' Julia confided, and Katy's heart stopped beating. 'But I was only very small, not very, very—wasn't I, Mum?'

'A bit small,' Katy agreed, as casually as she could. She might not be looking at Jake but his tension was transmitting itself in almost visible waves across the top of Julia's blonde head.

'That's why I'm blind,' the child added chirpily.

Katy heard the gasp as it escaped her lips. She knew Jake's footsteps had faltered but she still couldn't look at him. To see pity in his eyes would destroy the last shreds of her composure, and she couldn't let Julia realise how *distraite* she was.

'It was oxy—stuff to help me breathe that hurt my eyes,' Julia added, prattling on as if oblivious to the forces arcing through the air above her head.

'Oxygen?'

Jake offered the word gravely and Julia turned and smiled up at him.

'That's it!' she told him with transparent delight. 'Oxygen!'

But was she so oblivious? Or could she be carrying this conversation to help her mother out of what she sensed was an awkward encounter?

Katy shook her head, unable to think rationally about anything at the moment.

'It's this way,' she muttered when they reached the end of the lake. They turned towards the crossing that led to the road behind the hospital.

'These lights make a noise when it's safe to walk,' Julia confided to Jake. 'First you listen for the cars to stop, then you hear the noise that tells you when to cross.'

She let go of Katy's hand but kept hold of Jake's as she reached out for the smooth metal pole and felt for the button that would stop the traffic. Katy felt a pang of jealousy and told herself she was being ridiculous. Julia had a warm, open, loving nature. She adopted everyone she met as her friend.

'Come on, Mum,' she urged, and Katy took her hand again, scolded her for swinging on the road, then stopped when they'd made the safety of the opposite footpath.

'We go around the back,' she said to Jake, looking directly at him for the first time since they'd met beneath the trees. She hoped her face was as expressionless as his!

'Then you might show me the back way into this place,' he suggested. 'I had to pretend I was a cleaner to get safely through the crowd at the front door. I walked out with a fellow carrying a fearsome polishing machine and tried to look as if I knew exactly how it worked.'

Katy's lips twitched as she imagined the scene and she felt her muscles begin to relax, although she knew their relationship had taken yet another twist. Jake might have spoken lightly but there had been an edge to the words.

'Come on, then.' She led the way along the path to-wards the back of the old hospital building, where the crèche was situated.

'You mentioned fighting for the crèche,' Jake said as they walked into the brightly decorated yard and Julia was welcomed by her friends and whisked away from them. 'I didn't think!'

He stopped and looked around, and she knew his

mood had darkened with the swiftness of a sudden summer storm.

'I should have figured it out then! Talk about single-minded! Talk about not taking hints! I'm sorry, Katy!'

He sounded angry and upset, yet the apology was genuine.

But for what?

'Sorry, Jake?' she asked, and saw pain and a rueful kind of self-mockery in his eyes.

'Sorry for marching back into your life like this,' he pointed out. 'I assumed—'

He gave a bark of laughter and turned to walk away, but she caught his arm and stopped him.

'Assumed what?' she demanded. He'd already spoilt her morning, tied her nerves in knots and destroyed the fragile web of protection she'd woven around herself and Julia. She wasn't going to let him get away with more.

'Assumed because you weren't married you'd still be single! Stupid, wasn't I? I actually tracked you down, Katy. I phoned the General first and you weren't there. I tried St Christopher's, and then Lake Shore North. I was starting with the places close to your home—and, of course, I was looking for a nurse.'

He paused, but she knew he hadn't finished and she waited, bemused by the passion she could sense in him.

'When I learnt there was an admin assistant named Katy Turner here, I could have cried with relief, and then, when I found which department you worked for, I decided it was meant to be—that maybe I would be granted a second chance. I practically begged Dan Petersen to take that scholarship, and mortgaged my soul to get away from my other job. And all the time I had this weird idea that if I could only see you again, spend time with you, talk to you and try to explain, then maybe...'

Another hesitation, but this time Katy battled hope. If they talked...? If he could explain...?

'But of course marriage isn't everything these days. You found another man, you had a child—no wonder you didn't finish nursing! I assume he's still around, Katy? Assume the flowers were from him? What a bloody fool you must have thought me!'

He spun away again and this time she let him go, not bothering to remind him that he'd wanted to learn the back way into the hospital.

She found Julia and said goodbye to her. Jake had handed her a solution to her problem—a mythical man in her life. She doubted if this ghost would provide the buffer zone she needed between his body and hers, but it would stop his teasing comments and the remarks which suggested he was aware of her reaction to him.

She made her way up to the fourth floor, pausing in the foyer to speak to the security man on duty.

'We're managing,' he assured her. 'One woman reporter sneaked in in a nurse's uniform during the night, but Sister dealt with her. Pretended she thought she was a new nurse on the roster. She took her to the store cupboard, got out an enema tube and bowl and told her to do all the patients in 'C'. The silly nit nearly had a heart attack!'

He chuckled as he related the story, which must have spread through the hospital like wildfire. 'Even I know you don't give enemas any more—well, not *after* the baby's born, anyway.'

Katy smiled at his delight, then turned and made her way reluctantly towards her office.

You have to face him some time, she told herself. So he thinks you've got a lover! So what?

But she didn't have to face him. The room was empty and a note on her desk told her he was doing a postnatal clinic. She frowned at the note. Ron Spencer usually did the public postnatal clinics while private patients saw their own specialists. She made a mental note to ask about it, then attacked the day's work—beginning with a call to the nursery to check on staffing.

'We could do with someone willing to work split shifts,' Sue told her. 'Six to ten in the morning, and four to eight in the evenings. I can take an extra nurse off the wards from ten till four. Could you try Joe Cameron? He's worked with most of these nurses before and I'd like another male voice in the nursery.'

Katy smiled. Sue was adamant babies needed to hear and feel men as well as women tending them. Joe was a most unlikely nurse—a husky six-footer with a deep and unmistakably masculine voice. He was studying for a doctorate in nursing and took casual work to pay his bills.

'I'll try him first,' she promised Sue.

She contacted Joe and arranged for him to start that afternoon then left the office to check the cleaners had begun work in 'A'. She was tempted towards the nursery, but knew there was no real reason for her to go and peer at the new arrivals. And Mrs Carstairs had generated too much fuss for Katy to want to see her.

She spoke to Jenny, who was trying to keep the cleaners' noise to a minimum, then walked back to her office. Still no Jake!

It set the pattern for the days to come. He was out of the office more than he was in it and he treated her with a polite detachment when they were forced to speak about their work. She suspected he was feeling as much strain as she was, and was sometimes tempted to say, There's no one else. But that would lead her back into the limbo of doubt—the 'Should I? Shouldn't I?' state of indecision that was as dangerous as an unexploded bomb.

CHAPTER SEVEN

THEY kept up the pretence of a normal working relationship, helped by the chaos still erupting every day as a result of Mrs Carstairs and her hunger for publicity. As soon as she sensed interest in herself or the babies was dying down, she pulled a new stunt—for example she and Mr Carstairs, drawn together by this great event, reconfirming their marriage vows in the hospital suite, with television cameras and a viewing audience of millions.

'And she had the hide to ask Stewart Anderson to be a witness,' Jake fumed when he passed on this information to Katy.

Katy chuckled, but she was upset the chief medical officer at the hospital hadn't stepped in to stop these wilder examples of excess.

'It's the old story,' Jake said, once again plucking her thoughts out of the air. 'Any publicity is good publicity.'

'Not when it interferes with the running of the hospital and the comfort and security of other patients,' Katy objected. 'This is where private ownership of hospitals breaks down—the situation where service clashes with the profits.'

Jake shrugged.

'I agree, but it's hard to get that point across to the powers-that-be when the name of Lake Shore North is blazoned across the headlines each morning.'

But things did quieten a little after that, and she wondered if Jake had spoken to someone.

On Friday afternoon she handed him the list of objections she predicted Mr Forbes might raise.

'I'll go through them over the weekend,' he promised her, and her heart clenched at the sincerity in his voice. He might be regretting the wild impulse that had led him back to the past, but he would do his best for her.

'Thank you, Jake,' she said quietly, then turned away. She'd have liked to say something else, but Friday afternoons were always hurried. By the time she and Julia had walked home, discussing the day's happenings, then had a play, a bath and dinner, it would be time for Katy to get ready for her other job.

Besides, what was there she could say? Have a good weekend? When she knew he was practically a stranger here. He'd studied in Perth, coming east to do his residency—and back then they'd been a twosome, each to each other, all the friends either of them had wanted or needed.

She left him sitting at his desk, reading through her list. Would he work here for a few hours, then go upstairs to his room and order over-cooked steak from the canteen?

It's not your business what he does, she told herself as she left to collect Julia. Yet her heart ached to think he might be lonely. She thought of what he'd said about a school in holiday time and felt a similar emptiness, like hunger, hollowing out her body.

Julia was asleep by the time Katy said goodbye to Marie, her regular babysitter, and left to catch the bus into town. Leaving her daughter asleep soothed her conscience about working the two nights a week—at least Julia wasn't missing her!

The Baron's Table hadn't changed much in the ten years Katy had worked there. She'd gone south when

she was pregnant, needing to get away from both acquaintances and memories, but when she'd returned to
Lake Shore her job had been waiting for her, and she'd
found a babysitter and slipped easily back into her old
routine.

Tonight it was quiet, barely half-full, and she had time
to talk to her customers, catching up with the regulars'
news and fending off questions about the 'big event' at
the hospital.

At nine o'clock a group of eight came in and she was
suddenly busy. She had delivered one half of their order
and was heading back towards the kitchen for the re-
mainder when someone tapped her on the shoulder.

'Any chance of a medium rare steak in this place?'

She spun around and stared at Jake in disbelief.

'Well?' he prompted.

'Sit down and I'll get someone to take your order,'
she gabbled, unable to stop the rapid beating of her pulse
or a strange light-headed excitement.

Had he come on the off-chance that she might still
work at the same place? Or for nostalgic reasons? Or
simply because the restaurant was noted for its quality
food?

She sent a young waitress to his table, finished serving
her customers, then raced out to the office to find Ben
Logan, her boss, and one of the few people who knew
Jake was Julia's father.

'He doesn't know,' she told Ben, after explaining
about Jake's sudden re-emergence in her life, 'and I'm
not going to tell him.'

Ben frowned at her.

'I know he hurt you, Katy,' Ben murmured. 'Heaven
knows, I could have killed the bastard with my bare
hands he hurt you so bad. But don't you think he de-

serves to know he has a child? And, from a purely practical point of view, don't you think you could do with a little help from him financially?'

'No and no,' she said firmly. 'I tried to tell him once and he sent my letters back. Now, for Julia's sake if nothing else, it's best he doesn't know.'

Ben shrugged his shoulders.

'I won't say anything, then,' he muttered. 'In fact, I think I'll stay in here, then I don't have to talk to the guy. I might still feel the need to punch him in the jaw.'

Katy chuckled at the image of the short, tubby, dapper little restaurateur taking on the tall, well-muscled Jake.

'Perhaps I can stay in here with you?' Katy asked, only half-joking as she fought the physical effect of Jake's presence nearby.

Ben reached out and touched her hand.

'You'll cope, my girl,' he told her. 'You've the strength of a hundred tigers when it comes to something you really want to do—and a thousand tigers when it comes to that kid of yours!'

'That's what you think!' Katy muttered. 'At the moment a mouse could beat me—and an underfed mouse at that!'

She left the room and returned to her duties, studiously ignoring Jake, who was flirting with the young waitress and apparently enjoying his steak.

And his coffee! Then more coffee.

He was still sitting alone at his table when Katy went through to the cloakroom to change into her street clothes. She wondered if he'd arranged to take the younger waitress out for a drink when she finished work. The thought depressed her as she struggled into her jeans and pulled the zip up so forcefully it jammed and she had to fiddle with it to release it.

'Walk you to your car, lady?'

He was waiting by the door and she flinched away from him as he touched her arm. They walked through the door together, but she hesitated on the pavement. The flashing blue and red restaurant sign was turned off as they emerged and their eyes had to adjust to the shadowy darkness.

'I—I catch the bus,' she stuttered to break the sudden silence. He was suffocatingly close, and now even she could smell the drift of tangy aftershave Julia had associated with lemon grass. 'Just up the road.'

'Oh, for Pete's sake, Katy! Don't tell me you still rely on public transport? How do you get Julia to medical appointments? And don't bother telling me she doesn't have any! I'd have thought even a stubborn, independent woman like you would have realised the difference your own car could make.'

He drew her out of the way of a group of young people heading for the night-club up the road and she leant against the wall, trying to gather the strength to walk away from him.

'You work full time at a well-paid job and waitress at night. Why haven't you got a car?'

She smiled at his vehemence and shook her head as past and present collided again. Jake had wanted to buy her a car to help her cope with her hectic work and study schedule. He had always been infuriated by her determination to be independent.

'Same old arguments, huh, Jake?'

He dragged his fingers through his hair, tugging at it as if it might stimulate his brain.

'Same old lots of things, Katy,' he said soberly. 'I'd always thought desire was something cerebral—you liked someone so were physically attracted to them, as if there were a mental switch of some kind. But if that's the case, a person should be able to turn it off.'

He leaned closer, too close.

'Especially when one realises the object of desire isn't interested. Ridiculous, isn't it, that desire can still exist in such a vacuum? Such an unlikely situation?'

The words brushed across her lips in light puffs of air only seconds before his mouth closed on hers. Their noses bumped and she tilted her head to make the contact easier, forgetting she shouldn't be reacting, shouldn't be kissing him back with all the hunger of her love-parched soul.

Her arms crept around his shoulders, feeling the flesh and bone of him beneath the soft cotton shirt. Her fingers tangled in his hair where it brushed against his collar, then slid upwards to press against his scalp, cradling his head as they slaked their thirst for kisses.

Fine way of showing you're not interested! her mind yelled, while her body moulded itself closer to his. It was so good to be held against him, to feel complete again. Warmth filled her veins, saturating her senses, and a strange lightness made her cling more tightly to Jake, as if to anchor herself in some reality.

'Perhaps not a vacuum!' he murmured, and she shivered as the huskiness in his voice played its own part in her seduction.

His tongue skimmed across her lips, probed deeper, touched and taunted hers, and she stopped thinking altogether and gave herself up to the sensations that came flooding through her body, wave after wave of desire, and heat, and need.

She returned his kisses with a desperation born of six long years of separation. Somewhere in her mind a voice argued that it shouldn't be like this, that the magic shouldn't still be working after all this time! It must be lust! the voice insisted. A frustration-induced chemical reaction! A hormonal rush!

She ignored the voice and pressed closer, her hands conducting their own exploration while her lips tingled with the taste of him and her body throbbed beneath his hands.

'Let's find somewhere a little more private.'

Jake's voice, ragged with emotion, stilled her hands. They were inside his shirt, pressing on his skin, teasing at the whorls of hair and tight, nubby nipples. She withdrew them slowly and patted her own clothes into a semblance of order. She tried to stop the shaking, but no deep breaths or silent common-sense advice could still the raging tumult of her senses.

'Let's not,' she muttered, her own voice as hoarse and rasping as his had been. 'This is stupid, Jake. It can't happen. I can't let it happen!'

She pushed away from him and clutched her hands against her chest, hoping pressure might calm the turmoil surging beneath her skin.

'Why not, Katy?' he asked, his fingers smoothing her tangled hair back from her face, touching her skin with the lightness of love.

But was it love? Or that far more inconvenient emotion, passion? Hadn't she mistaken passion for love once before, then felt the fury of the flames as it had burnt itself out?

'Because of Julia's father?' he demanded gruffly.

'N-no!' she stuttered, then registered who Julia's father was and amended her answer to a frantic, 'Yes!'

'You can't love him and respond to me as you did!' Jake growled, clasping her shoulders as if he'd like to shake some sense into her. 'If you're sticking with him

for Julia's sake, it's a big mistake, Katy. You, of all
people, should know that. Think what happened in your
life because of misguided choices.'

Her own childhood was the last thing she wanted to
consider at the moment. Jake's anger was as potent as
his kisses—because it made it seem as if he cared! She
shivered in the darkness as he spoke again.

'And what is he? Some worthless scum who can't
afford to keep you? He bloody well can't think much of
you to let you work the hours you work—and as for
letting you travel on public transport at this time of the
night—!'

'Hear, hear!' a male voice responded, and Katy spun
around.

Jake's complaints, growing louder with each griev-
ance, had attracted the attention of passers-by so they
now had a small crowd of onlookers.

'Well, I can't take public transport tonight,' she
pointed out. 'You've made me miss my bus!'

Her voice was shaking as much as her body, and she
leaned back against the wall and tried deep breaths
again.

'Drive her home, mate!' one of the strangers encour-
aged, and Katy, infuriated to find she'd become a bit of
sidewalk entertainment, turned on Jake.

'I'd rather walk!' she snapped, and whirled to face the
spectators. 'And the show's over, so you can all go
home!'

'We're not going home!' one of the girls said. 'It's
only one o'clock. We're going to the Night Owl—why
don't you come along? A few drinks—bit of danc-
ing—sort out your problems in a civilised atmosphere.'

Someone giggled and Katy realised their audience had
already had a few drinks—enough to mellow them, to

let them think they could solve the problems of the entire world.

The anger trickled out of her as she remembered feeling that way herself, then she felt Jake's arm reach out and draw her close.

'Not tonight,' he said gruffly. 'But I hope you all enjoy yourselves.'

Katy swallowed, trying to banish silly tears that had welled up at this new memory of the past—and of the dark, underground club where she and Jake had danced till dawn the evening of the day they'd met. It had become 'their' place, frequented on the nights when they didn't have work commitments or early-morning schedules.

'Come on,' he said when the group had wandered off. 'I don't have a car to run you home but I'll put you in a cab. I'll even pay for it, as I've made you miss your bus!'

He sounded tired but his arm still held her close. As he steered her along the footpath she didn't pull away from him but relished the warmth of his body against hers—even if it was only as far as the cab rank.

'Will you go up to the Night Owl on your own?' she asked. 'Or there's a new place near City Square called Four Bells. A lot of the hospital staff go there—I believe it's very nice.'

'You sound like a tour guide,' he said gruffly. 'I don't need entertainment or night-clubs or social meetings with other staff, Katy. I'll put you in a cab and take the next one on the rank straight back to the hospital.'

'That's ridiculous,' she protested. 'If we're going the same way we can share a cab.'

She felt the movement of his muscles as he shrugged, then his arm dropped from her shoulders as they reached the first cab in the rank. He leant forward and opened the door for her, told the driver to head along Lake Shore Drive towards the hospital, then dropped into the darkness beside her. Without thinking, she reached out and took hold of his hand.

They sat in silence as the cab left the city. Jake's fingers lay passively in hers yet she fancied she could feel the blood running through them, keeping his precious flesh alive. She brushed her thumb across his skin, warm, satiny skin, and remembered how his chest had felt—the coarseness of the hair.

She'd splayed her fingers in it in the past, reaching out before she went to sleep as if the physical connection with Jake would keep her safe throughout the night. In the morning, she would feel him move, and wake to turn into his arms...

'Turn here. It's the second house on the left,' she told the cab driver, shunning the memories.

The security light above her front door flashed on as the cab registered on the sensor.

Katy hesitated, reluctant to leave the cocoon of darkness, then, obeying instinct rather than common-sense, she leaned sideways and kissed Jake softly on the lips.

'Goodnight!' she murmured, then she opened the door and slid out before she did anything else she was certain to regret later.

Marie was awake, head bent over books and papers spread across Katy's dining table.

'Busy night?' she asked, without raising her eyes from her work.

'Not bad!' Katy told her. 'Want tea or coffee?'

Marie shook her head, and Katy remembered her own absorption with study when she'd been Marie's age. She and Jake would begin together, but his brain worked faster than hers and he'd finish his allotted amount of work and then pace around the room, trying to tempt her away from her set task.

She shook her head, remembering the feel of his fingers in her hair, his lips on the nape of her neck—then the shivering torment as she tried to deny the effect he had on her!

'I'm going up to bed. Don't overdo it!' she said, as she always did. She was halfway up the steps before her words registered with Marie, who called a belated goodnight in an abstracted voice.

Katy reached the landing and turned towards Julia's room. Her daughter lay face-down, flung across the bed as if sleep had caught her by surprise and tossed her there. Katy smoothed the golden hair and pulled a sheet over the slight body. She turned down the covers on the second bed. Marie would creep in later and sleep through half the day, relishing the quiet of Katy's home.

Thinking about the luxury of sleeping in made Katy yawn. She tiptoed out of the room and headed for her bedroom. Julia would be shaking her awake in less than four hours—sleep-ins existed only in her dreams!

Their Saturday morning routine involved getting several loads of washing onto the line—a task that was becoming increasingly difficult as Julia grew older and insisted on helping. That done, the two of them headed for the shops, Julia dragging the wheeled trolley on the way there, and Katy pushing it, full of groceries, on the way back.

After lunch they walked down to the lake, where they fed the swans and played games identifying people by the way they walked, or through snippets of the conversations which reached their ears.

It was a good game because Julia insisted Katy close her eyes. This meant she could lie on the blanket, put her hat over her face, and doze between passers-by.

'It's the new doctor from the hospital,' Julia hissed, rolling over on the blanket so her lips were close to Katy's ear.

'You can't know that,' Katy told her, too tired to stir.

'I do, I do!' Julia insisted, then she moved away and Katy, reaching out and not making contact, sat up with a start.

'Good afternoon, ladies!'

Katy felt her spine stiffen and tiny tendrils of delight flicker in her blood.

'It can't be!' she wailed, watching as he bent and touched her daughter on the shoulder.

'Can't be me? This park private?'

His eyes were wary, gazing down at her over Julia's tumbled curls. Such lovely eyes...

She shook away the fancies. This intuitive process of Julia's was becoming too unsettling for her to be thinking of blue eyes.

'I can't tell how she knows!' she told him, while Julia tugged on his hand, urging him to join them on the blanket.

Which wasn't that good an idea, Katy realised, as the blanket shrank to pocket handkerchief size.

'Other senses compensate,' Jake reminded her, taking Julia in his arms and settling her on his knee.

'You try it! Go on! Lie down and close your eyes and listen to the footsteps of people going past. What can you tell about them?'

'Yes, do it, Dr Cartwright,' Julia urged, standing up so she could push at his shoulders and force him backwards.

He gave in to her insistence, making her gurgle with delight when he tumbled over, pretending he was too weak to resist her.

His head came to rest on Katy's thigh, but when she tried to move she found her muscles wouldn't respond to her command, so he lay there, eyes closed, allowing her to study his dear, familiar face. Strong-jawed, harsh-profiled, it was a manly juxtaposition of features that was uniquely Jake—uniquely charming, and very, very sexy.

She clenched her hands, feeling her fingernails biting into her palms as she resisted the urge to run them across his smooth, tight skin and feel the ridges of bone that shaped his looks.

'Someone's coming,' Julia warned, tucking her body close to Jake's and taking his hand in hers.

'It's a man,' Jake guessed. 'And he's plump and most important because he walks with short, strutting kinds of steps. I think he's wearing a red waistcoat, yellow tie, blue suit and carrying a red and yellow umbrella.'

Julia clapped her delight.

'Is he right, Mum, is he right?' she asked, squirming with excitement.

'Almost right,' Katy told her, as an elderly man in grey shorts and a blue shirt ambled by. 'Except his waistcoat's blue and the umbrella is purple.'

'Not true!' Julia declared. 'He smelled like onions, and I'm sure an onion man wouldn't carry a purple umbrella.'

Jake sat up slowly, and Katy was fairly certain he was sniffing the air.

'How often is she right?' he asked, his fingers stroking Julia's arm absent-mindedly.

'If it's someone we know—'

'Like my babysitter, Marie, or Nan, or her family, or Helen from the hospital—' Julia interjected.

'Almost always,' Katy finished. 'She told me you were here, but, as she's only met you once, I didn't believe it. I keep wondering if she might be... If I should...'

Her voice trailed away a second time. She couldn't voice her concerns in front of Julia, but if she could talk to Jake about the possibility that her child was especially gifted he might be able to advise her on whether it was important to have her tested.

'Are you working tonight?' he asked, and Julia replied for her.

'Mum's always working!'

Katy knew the disapproval in her voice was a bit of child-parent manipulation, but she couldn't help defending herself.

'I don't leave till you're asleep,' she pointed out. 'It's not as if you're missing out on special time with me.'

'But you're tired next day,' Julia continued, obviously pleased to have a new audience for her complaints.

'Enough!' Katy told her. 'We've been through all this before.'

'But I haven't,' Jake objected. 'I'm with Julia. I'd like to know why you have to work nights—why you're still pushing yourself so hard?'

He sat up and turned so he was facing her, and she found it difficult to meet his eyes.

'We're paying off the house and Mum's saving for my new computer,' Julia answered, before Katy realised her daughter was still involved in the conversation. 'Mum says she's sure a spaceship would be cheaper, but a spaceship wouldn't be nearly as much fun for me as a computer that talks.'

Katy saw Jake's eyes darken with anger and she could read the unspoken question.

Does her father provide nothing? he was silently demanding, but, 'Why, Katy, why?' was all he said.

Julia decided the question was meant for her and launched into a list of the virtues of her computer. Katy turned away, looking out across the lake to where the two swans glided, their growing brood holding a straight line behind them.

Soon the park rangers would take the young swans away. Would the parents assume their children had willingly left the nest? Taken off because it was time to go? Her own experience of family was so bizarre she found it hard to judge even the feathered variety.

'Swans stay together for ever.'

Julia's clear, childish voice, adopting a different subject but one still close to her heart, brought her back to earth with a jolt.

'The mother and father, that is,' she added. 'The children leave home when they're old enough, but the mother and father stay together.'

Katy knew the heat she felt must have turned her cheeks to scarlet. So many conversations coming back to haunt her! Jake had told her about the swans and she'd argued from her own experience, using the words he'd repeated to her last night, that staying together wasn't always so good.

'It's because they love each other,' her parrot of a daughter added. 'It only works with the love bit, Mum says.'

'Does she, pet?' Jake said lightly, but Katy could hear the pressure of her own tears in his voice.

'We've got to go!' she announced, standing up so

suddenly her calf muscles cramped and she stumbled awkwardly.

Jake reached out to steady her, and, looking down, she saw more questions in his eyes. He rose to his feet but she couldn't bring herself to step away from him, so their clothes and skin brushed against each other and tremors of excitement fluttered in her lungs.

If she touched him now...

If he took her arm...

'Can I run?'

She caught back the drifting, dangerous thoughts and turned towards her daughter, poised at the junction between the two paths.

'As far as the shadows,' Katy told her, and watched the slender figure dart towards the trees.

'I make sure there are no pedestrians to be knocked over,' she explained to Jake, her voice as hoarse as if it were never used.

'Has she enough sight to tell where the shadows begin?' he asked, damping down her erratic reaction with the practicality of the question.

'I don't think so.' She gathered up the blanket and walked towards her waiting daughter. 'I think she can tell by the change in temperature on her skin. I don't like to probe too much in case...' She hesitated, wondering how she could explain her reservations. 'When you were a kid, did you ever wake up in the night and think you'd forgotten how to breathe? It's such an automatic action no one analyses it, yet when you start to think about it, you find it difficult.'

His footsteps slowed, as if he knew she would want to finish this conversation before they reached Julia.

'You're afraid if she starts to think about how she senses things, she'll lose the knack?'

'Exactly! So I bumble along, wondering about it, trying desperately to train my senses in the same way—to find some clue of how things work for her.'

'It would be an interesting study—the degree of sensory perception in sight or hearing-impaired children.'

'Wouldn't it just?' Katy agreed fervently. They reached Julia and she took her by the hand. 'It's one of my dreams,' she confessed, adding, in almost inaudible tones, 'One day!'

She felt Jake's attention shift, and wondered if he was thinking of a similar dream she'd shared with him. I'll be a nurse—one day! She straightened her shoulders, arguing silently against an imagined reminder. Just because one dream had died, it didn't mean you held a wake for all the others!

He walked with them to the end of the avenue of trees.

'We're going swimming in the hospital pool tomorrow morning,' Julia told him, while Katy wondered why she'd spent so much money on speech therapy because she'd been worried about Julia's verbalisation skills. At the moment she could see unlimited advantages in having a non-verbal child! 'Because you're a doctor, you could come.'

'That would be lovely,' he said gravely. 'If I'm not working, I'd like to join you.'

'And have lunch with us afterwards in the canteen?' Julia urged, and as Jake raised that questioning eyebrow at her Katy shrugged.

'She especially loves their mushy beans on toast—prefers the canteen to McDonalds.'

He looked horrified—probably remembering the steak—but he made a noise that could have been a yes, then touched his new admirer lightly on the head.

'See you in the pool, Julia,' he said. 'Be good.'

'I'm always good,' she told him indignantly. 'I'm my Mum's one and only best, best girl!'

Katy saw Jake straighten and his eyes met hers. Her heart thundered as she realised how many 'Jakisms' she had unconsciously passed on to Julia, including 'You're my one and only best, best girl'. Would he remark on it? She waited, feeling the silence, like the sunshine, on her skin.

'I'm on call, and the place is still a mad house, so I'll be at the hospital if you want to talk to me,' was all he said, then he turned and walked away.

What did he mean—want to talk to him? Surely he couldn't have picked up anything about her single state from Julia's prattling conversation. For one horrible moment Katy had thought Julia might blurt out the information that her father hadn't loved her mother, which was why, unlike the swans, her parents had parted. But she'd been diverted in time, so it couldn't be that!

CHAPTER EIGHT

JAKE wasn't at the pool, but Helen was enjoying the use of the hospital facilities and she filled Katy in on the latest drama being played out in the main building.

'Happened in the early hours of this morning,' she began, settling herself on the edge of the pool where Katy sat to watch Julia swim back and forth across the width. 'Post-partum haemorrhage! You can imagine the scene. Mr Carstairs, who's usually very meek and mild, screaming hysterically at the sight of blood, and Mrs Carstairs—predictably—threatening to sue everyone from the hospital shareholders to the security guards.'

'Was Dr Anderson available?' Katy asked, and saw Helen shake her head.

'When's a specialist ever around when you need him? He was at his daughter's wedding down the coast, but Jake Cartwright was on call and fortunately lives in the hospital. He appeared within minutes and told Mrs Carstairs he'd let her bleed to death if she didn't stop her nonsense.'

Katy whirled on her friend, shock jolting her upright.

'He couldn't possibly have said anything so stupid! "Never make even light-hearted threats to patients!" That's rammed into every nursing and medical student from the time they start to study.'

'Well,' Helen said, 'he didn't quite use those words, but I think he got the message across that if she continued to make a fuss, things could get worse. Anyway, according to the night staff, she settled down.'

Helen kicked at the water, sending an arc of droplets into the air. 'Mind you, I suspect that man could charm the flowers off wallpaper if he set his mind to it,' she added.

'What was the problem?' Katy asked, hiding the strange scrunchy feeling she felt inside when Helen spoke of Jake.

'Well, it could have been retained placental material or uterine atony—the uterus not contracting properly after the birth. Usually that shows up sooner, but it wouldn't be surprising after the stretching it must have had during Mrs Carstairs's pregnancy. She'd been given the usual dosage of oxytocin in IV fluids after the placenta was delivered, and the staff had been massaging her when she'd allow it—'

'You mean when she wasn't busy giving interviews or getting remarried!' Katy had seen the list of 'appointments' Mrs Carstairs had arranged through her publicity managers.

Helen laughed, agreeing that the whole procedure had been stage-managed throughout.

'Anyway, Dr Cartwright told her if it was that, there were two options: drugs or surgery. You can imagine how she reacted to any suggestion of surgery! He palpated her abdomen and decided it was boggy enough to need dealing with first, so he increased the infusion rate, added Methergine sequentially and everyone waited.'

'Methergine?' Katy repeated the unfamiliar word.

'It'll usually produce really strong uterine contractions—some specialists use it, some prostoglandin. I've known them to use both in quite a few cases. I think Dr Cartwright was a bit doubtful about the effectiveness of drugs, with the patient's abdomen the way it was and the possibility that the haemorrhage might have been caused by something else. Anyway, she's got blood replacement flowing into one arm and the IV cocktail into the other, and she must have felt a bit better because she demands we get the photographer and video cameraman back in to record this bit of the drama for posterity.'

'I don't believe you,' Katy gasped. 'She must still have been feeling dreadful—why would she want anyone taking films or photographs?'

'Why would she do any of the things she's done?' Helen asked. 'I'm just glad I wasn't on duty! Evidently Dr Cartwright blew his top and told her she was a seriously ill woman and he was going to invoke hospital regulations to prevent anyone other than her husband entering her room.'

'Can we do that? *Are* there hospital regulations which give us such power?'

'Ron Spencer asked him that when they walked out of her room, and Ron says Dr Cartwright said he'd make some up if necessary, but he was damned if he was going to lose a patient because some press hound wanted one last photo. Seems he sent people flying in all directions—wanted new blood tests for a coagulation profile, ultrasound for retained placental material or blood-clots—'

Julia swam back to where the two women sat, bobbed her head above water, grabbed Katy's ankle and demanded, 'Where's my doctor?'

'She's met Dr Cartwright,' Katy explained to Helen, then she touched Julia on the head and said, 'He's very busy today.'

Seemingly satisfied, Julia felt along the edge of the pool beside where Katy sat, finally locating four thick plastic hoops. She positioned herself carefully, her back against her mother, and dropped them into the water so they formed a semi-circle around her feet on the bottom of the pool.

'Now, I'll dive for them,' she announced.

'She's showing off for you, seeing ''her'' doctor isn't here,' Katy explained to Helen. She watched Julia's legs thresh above the water as she duck-dived to the bottom, but her mind was on Jake and the problems he'd been having.

'What did the scan show? Did he take her back to Theatre for a curette?' she asked, reaching out to take the first coloured hoop from Julia. 'Very smart!' she told her daughter, and watched her dive again.

'Unfortunately it was unclear. No nice line showing the uterus had contracted, and little sign of anything else. He suggested a curette, in case that was the problem, but she refused to consider his performing even such a simple operation. She wanted Anderson or no one, and refused to give consent.'

'Poor Jake!' Katy murmured, taking the second hoop from Julia.

She felt a shift in Helen's attention and heard a hint of added interest when she said, 'You sound as if you really care!'

'I care about any doctor who's given a hard time by a patient. When things go wrong, they have to cop both the patient's blame and their own uneasiness that they might have been able to do more. In cases like this, the doctor is in a rotten situation.'

'I guess!' Helen murmured, but she didn't sound as if she was thinking about Mrs Carstairs.

Julia picked up the last two hoops.

'Time to get out, kitten,' Katy said to her. 'You're getting waterlogged.'

'Once more, over and back,' Julia pleaded.

'Okay, see how quickly you can swim.'

'She's so fearless,' Helen remarked. 'She splashes into people, then gets going again as if she can actually see the other side of the pool.'

'I know she can distinguish light and dark,' Katy explained, 'but I'm beginning to wonder if she can also detect some difference in the texture of the light. So the other side of the pool might have a particular appearance she can recognise.'

'Have you had her tested?' Helen asked, and Katy shook her head.

'You and Nan!' she muttered. 'You're both as bad as each other. What if I do have her tested and it proves she's in the group they class as "talented and gifted"? What's it going to prove? The special clubs and programmes they have are for sighted kids.'

'As long as I've known you, Katy, you've never treated Julia as if she's sight-impaired. Why would joining one of those groups make a difference?'

'I can't explain,' Katy told her. 'I haven't said I *won't* have her tested—I'm still thinking about it.'

She knew she sounded defensive, but she remembered Jake telling her about the club he'd attended. His intelligence had made him 'different' from the other kids at his school, and he'd had to play harder and fight tougher and continually prove himself as 'normal' as any of his peers, again and again.

And Julia was already 'different'.

She helped her daughter out of the pool and wrapped a towel, cloak-like, around her, wishing she had the power to provide a cloak of emotional protection as easily.

'See you tomorrow,' she said to Helen, herding Julia towards the changing rooms. They'd have lunch in the canteen then walk home, and, with any luck, Julia would sleep for a few hours and she could lie down and relax herself. Her quiet Sunday afternoons were precious—a time when she was just herself, not an administrator, or a waitress, or Julia's mother.

James Carlyle, the chief medical officer at the hospital, put paid to that plan. The phone was ringing when they reached home.

'Can you come in to work, Katy? There's all hell breaking loose in this place and I need someone to man the phone on your ward. Three of the staff have already been reduced to tears after they refused to give out information and the switchboard operators are threatening to quit if they have to handle all the calls themselves.'

He sounded tired and harassed.

'I've spoken to Nan Chalmers from the crèche and told her we need you here. She suggested you take a cab and drop Julia at her place. Charge it to the hospital, of course.'

'Okay, James,' she agreed. 'I'll get there as quickly as I can.'

Given Mrs Carstairs's propensity for publicity, she didn't know why she was surprised to hear that this latest dramatic development had been made public. No doubt the woman would milk it for all it was worth.

Julia was playing on the floor, rolling balls with one hand and catching them with the other.

'I've got to go to work for a while, pet. Would you mind if I dropped you at Nan's place?'

Silly question! Julia loved going to Nan's—in fact, her enjoyment of the rough and tumble she shared with Nan's kids sometimes made Katy feel guilty about her daughter's only child status.

She phoned for a cab, then, leaving Julia playing, raced upstairs and threw some clean clothes for her daughter into a small backpack. Nan would keep her for the night if Katy was held up at the hospital, and the supply of clothes already at Nan's might not be enough.

She thought about changing out of her shorts, then decided no one would be worried about how she looked. She'd be a voice on the end of the phone, nothing more.

Nan was waiting on the footpath outside her place when the cab drew up. Katy kissed her daughter and handed her over, then climbed back into the vehicle.

The cab driver refused to be intimidated by the crush of people outside the main entrance to the hospital. He put his hand on the horn and blasted his way through towards the door.

'Charge it to the hospital, love?' he asked, and Katy agreed, giving him her authorisation number. She opened the door and leapt out, hoping she'd be taken for a normal visitor.

As she hurried past the security men who held the crowds at bay, she heard whispers of the stories that had swelled their ranks.

'Mother's dying…'

'Could be dead already…'

'Three babies gone…'

'Adoption…'

'No, all the babies are okay—the father says he'll bring them up himself. Someone's raising money…'

How do these rumours start? she wondered as she showed her identification to a policeman who was on duty in the main foyer.

James must be panicking to have brought in the law!

She found another policeman on the fourth floor and wondered what effect this circus was having on their other patients. And what did the Asian mothers, who turned shyly away from fuss and attention, make of it all?

She reached her office and phoned through to the switchboard to let them know she was there.

'Before you start directing calls to me, I'll need to speak to a doctor so I know exactly what I can and can't say,' she explained.

'Dr Anderson's not here yet, although I believe he's on his way,' the operator told her. 'I'll see if I can get on to Dr Cartwright or Dr Spencer.'

A few minutes later Ron Spencer knocked on the door.

'Thank goodness you're here, Katy. Maybe you can provide a bit of sanity in this madhouse.'

He perched on the edge of her desk, where Jake had sat.

The phone rang and she reached out to silence it.

'Could you hold for a minute?' she said politely, then flipped a switch so soothing music would play in the caller's ear. 'What's happening, Ron? And how much do we make public?'

'She's still bleeding, blood pressure's low. Jake's beside himself and someone is keeping sections of the media up to date on every move we make.'

'Can't we remove the phone from her suite on the pretext she's too sick to take calls?'

'We've done that,' he told her. 'There's another leak somewhere.'

'So what do we do?' she asked him.

'Take the calls and say she's stable. You can repeat that there's been some post-partum problems which are being handled in the usual manner.'

She lifted her eyebrow and he laughed.

'You'll think of something to keep them happy,' he assured her.

'I'll try,' she promised. 'But if word's leaking out somewhere else, you might put someone on to finding where. The rumours circulating downstairs are unbelievable.'

'I'll see what I can do,' he promised, and turned to leave.

Katy was about to switch back to the caller when she remembered the babies.

'What's the status of the kids?' she called after him, and he swung back towards her and shrugged.

'Go with "stable", Katy,' he said quietly. 'The neonatal specialist is still worried about two of them, and you know how dicey it is to predict outcomes for any pre-term baby.'

Katy watched him leave, then turned her attention to the caller. It was a reporter from an international newsgathering service who thought her charm and persistence would find a weakness in Katy's carefully worded statements. Katy fended her off, but she was relieved when the call was over. Until the next one came in! The switchboard must have had a backlog of them, for no sooner did she hang up than the phone would ring again.

Someone brought her a cup of tea, and Ron poked his head in at one stage to say there was no change but Stewart Anderson had finally arrived. A wardsmaid brought her a sandwich and she ate it while she talked, repeating over and over again the limited litany of facts.

At seven o'clock, James Carlyle came in.

'Come on, Katy, I'll drive you home.'

She'd been warily eyeing the phone, wondering why it hadn't rung for three minutes, and she looked up in surprise.

'Siege over?' she asked.

He nodded.

'I've given orders to the switchboard to tell all callers that this hospital will issue a news bulletin at seven tomorrow morning and no further information on the Carstairs' family is available until that time. I've also instructed the people on duty to hang up if a caller persists.'

'Good for you!' Katy applauded, knowing how wary James usually was about taking a firm stand with the press. He hated to think anything he said or did might dim the shining reputation of 'his' hospital.

'Yes, well...' he said, looking a little embarrassed by her mild praise. 'We discovered Mrs Carstairs's sister, who's been with her since she was admitted, has a cellular phone. She's the one who's been relaying all the information, slipping into the bathroom to make her calls. We can't stop her visiting her sister, nor can we prevent her using her own phone, but let's see what happens when word leaks out that she's the only contact. My guess is, she'll turn the damn thing off.'

Katy smiled at him.

'And will word leak out?' she asked.

'Just about now, I would say,' James told her, and moved towards the window. 'We can't see from here, but Jake Cartwright is about to do his "cleaner" routine and walk out muttering about how impossible it is to get work done in the place and fancy having to phone Miss Johnson's mobile to get access to the Carstairs room. As Miss Johnson featured largely in the television presentation of the birth, it shouldn't take the media people too long to work it out—or find out the number.'

'I could print it on a placard and hang it out the window if you like,' Katy suggested, wondering if Jake had thought of the plan to relieve pressure on the hospital phone lines.

James smiled at her.

'Let's hope that won't be necessary,' he said. 'Now, shall we go?'

For a moment she hesitated. While she'd been in the office there'd always been a chance Jake would call in for a few minutes and she'd see him. Now she was stupidly disappointed because he hadn't. She wouldn't even see him in the corridor or ward foyer if he was parading downstairs in disguise.

'Okay,' she agreed, hoping James didn't sense the reluctance in her voice.

Jake rang at nine, his voice a husky murmur over the phone, as if all his energy had drained away and the sounds were being formed by memory, not effort.

'I heard you'd been seconded this afternoon, but by the time I came up to see you James had whisked you away. Did you handle it okay, Katy?' he asked, his voice so flat she guessed he was depressed as well as tired.

'My job was the easy part,' she told him. 'How are you coping?'

'Just!' he muttered.

There was a pause, and then he said, 'Talk to me, Katy?'

She knew then that he'd rung because talking to her had, in the past, helped him think things through. He wouldn't talk about his problem right away, but would order her to talk while his mind sorted it into order. She began to speak, telling him of their trip to the pool, of Julia's diving for the rings.

'You were going to ask me something about her yesterday—about her sensory perception,' he reminded her. 'Want to ask me now?'

She would have loved to talk about it now, but would discussing Julia's abilities and reminding Jake of his own 'special' status link him to her in such a way he'd suspect their relationship? Just at the moment she couldn't think through all the implications of that particular discovery!

'No, I'll sort it out. She missed you at the pool,' Katy added, and heard him sigh.

'And you, Katy? Did you miss me?'

'Helen was there,' she said, skirting the question. 'She told me of your fun and games so I knew what was going on before James rang.'

They'd come full circle now. Was he ready for questions? She took a deep breath, then asked anyway. 'How's Mrs Carstairs?'

'Stewart Anderson is back, thank heavens,' Jake replied. 'He's with her now. The drugs weren't working and surgery is the only answer. He'll try tying off blood vessels, but, given the suspected severity of the atony, he may have to opt for a hysterectomy. He mentioned that possibility to Mrs Carstairs, and she's dug her heels in and refuses to allow him to take her to Theatre.'

'Is a hysterectomy such a problem? She's got five babies—surely that's enough for any woman?'

Another sigh filtered into her ear.

'You'd think so!' he said. 'Unfortunately I rather suspect she's had so much fun with all the publicity she wants to do it again. Although with new guidelines about fewer fertilised eggs being implanted the possibility of another multiple birth is unlikely.'

'But no one would put her on another IVF programme,' Katy protested. 'It would be...'

'Unethical?' he suggested. She could almost see the shrug which would have accompanied the word. 'The problems of ethics and IVF are so immense we haven't begun to sort them out. There are ethical and legal battles raging in countries all over the world over the destruction of frozen embryos. And, if you consider that a doctor should do his best to comply with the wishes of his patient, would it be so unethical to put Mrs Carstairs on another course of fertility drugs?'

'Yes!' Katy replied without the slightest hesitation. 'The programme was initiated for couples who had problems conceiving. There are waiting lists of people wanting to get on to the programme at Lake Shore North. If it had been a single birth, then fair enough—put her on the bottom of the list and let her work her way up to the top for a second child—'

'Hey, I happen to agree!' he interrupted, and his voice had lost the strain she'd detected earlier. In fact, he was probably laughing at her vehemence. 'But Mrs Carstairs still has the right to refuse surgery—for whatever reason—and so far that's exactly what she's doing.'

Katy groaned with disbelief.

'I'm glad I'm not a doctor,' she said. 'How can you hold back when you know the patient may die if you don't operate?'

'With a great deal of difficulty, Katy!'

There was a moment's silence, then he went on, 'I'll have to go back down to the ward and see what's happening. Thanks to you, my best, best girl, at least I feel halfway normal again.'

Her heart contracted, but she knew she couldn't let him get away with it.

'I'm not your girl, Jake,' she said quietly, denying her heart.

'No, Katy?' he murmured. 'Are you quite sure of that?'

'I have to be sure,' she told him sadly. 'Good luck!'

She turned on the television news next morning and learnt, with the rest of the population, that Mrs Carstairs had experienced some post-partum problems, had had some minor surgery and was resting comfortably. All five babies were progressing in a satisfactory manner.

James Carlyle had faced the cameras himself, and his calm demeanour had come across more strongly than the media's emotive questions, defusing much of the hype that had been associated with the Carstairs' family since before the birth.

Katy headed for work, hopeful that sanity would have been restored. She wanted the upperlevel powers in the hospital to be thinking about her new unit today, not about quintuplets. As she walked along beside the lake she hid a sense of disappointment that Jake hadn't come to meet her. It was stupid to feel that way, because she knew how hectic his weekend had been.

But he was in the office—standing just inside the door! She jolted to a stop and stared at him, transported back to Saturday night, when they'd kissed. Memory fired her blood.

'Still not my best, best girl?' he murmured, then he moved so his foot kicked the door closed. His hands grasped her shoulders and his lips met hers in a kiss of such hunger she gave herself up to the reaction she'd denied him a week ago.

Every cell in her body came to life—completely, joyously, throbbingly alive. She moved so their bodies fitted, complementing yet completing each other, and when the emotion he aroused began to drain the strength from her legs she let him ease her back against the closed door and hold her, so her body seemed suspended in the same unreality as time.

Then the phone rang, his pager bleeped, and her speaker phone told her she was needed in 'B'. Somehow the combination of demands broke through the spell and they released each other slowly, moving automatically to silence the ringing and buzzing.

She answered the phone, assured Sue Gates she could keep the extra staff and was heading for the door to answer the call to 'B' when Jake spoke.

'You can't love him, Katy!'

She turned back and frowned, wondering what on earth he was talking about.

'Julia's father!'

Oh, but I do, she thought, and panic began to shiver through her body.

It was like standing on the edge of a landslide—feeling that first downward slip and knowing if you turned around, if you tried to go back, half the hillside was likely to come tumbling down on top of you. Only it was Julia's happiness which could come tumbling down!

'I've got to go,' she mumbled, and hurried from the room.

Helen wanted some information on a patient dredged up from records. The woman had given birth in the hospital eight years ago and the records were no longer in the computer's data bank.

'I hate to ask you to do it, but the woman's in labour now and she's sure she had some problem last time but can't remember what,' Helen said. 'I rang Records and they've three staff off with the summer 'flu that's going around, and because it's a manual search they won't be able to get the information to me until later in the day.'

'I'll go down and see what I can find,' Katy told her, taking the slip of paper Helen handed her with the patient's details on it.

She made her way down to the records room in the basement of the newer part of the building. She'd worked here when she'd first come to Lake Shore North, so was familiar with the quiet surroundings.

The rooms were well sealed and air-conditioned, the temperature and humidity maintained at a set level to protect the records. They were stored on disk here, although Katy knew abbreviated hard copies were also kept in a second room.

She found the disk she needed, popped it into a computer and scanned it for the information she wanted. Information was cross referenced, so you could follow up an admittance date, a name, or even a condition. She used the search command and found the woman's name.

She was right when she said she'd had problems! There'd been a secondary arrest of dilation during her active labour, when dilation of the cervix had ceased for three hours. The doctor in charge had diagnosed inadequate uterine contractions rather than malposition of the foetus or foetal disproportion. He had allowed the patient to rest, then augmented the labour with oxytocin and the patient had delivered vaginally.

Katy typed in a 'print' command, and while she waited for the machine to spit out the information for Helen she studied the disk cabinets lining the walls—each year with its own divisions into departments. Obstetrics, Gynaecology, Neurology, Orthopaedics.

Orthopaedics! Jake had been in this hospital—his record would be in there.

Why should she care?

She couldn't answer, but knew she wanted desperately

to see his name, to read the medical description of that time of such great pain.

She glanced towards the printer, which was still chattering busily, then crossed to the file drawer for the year of the accident. She found the disk and slipped it into a second computer, again using 'search' to find Jake's name. As the bare clinical details rolled down the screen she recalled the shock and pain—even the sterility of the air in the ICU.

Head wound, mangled hip, fractured left femur, tibia and fibula, spinal cord compression, lacerations—

Spinal cord compression?

She went back and found the reference, demanding more information. Paralysis of lower limbs, word after word that meant little to her now, descriptions of tests carried out, of the lack of response to stimuli.

And three final words—'possible outcome paraplegia'.

'I had my reasons!'

Jake's voice echoed in her head, but the anguish she'd felt for him back then was blown apart by anger. She shut down the program, slammed the disk back into place, tore the reams of patient information from the printer and raced out of the room. Then she remembered the second disk and returned, telling herself to calm down. With shaking fingers she exited the program then returned the file.

Helen thanked her for her help, but Katy barely heard the words. She wanted to get back to her office and confront Jake Cartwright—confront him with his cowardice. For that was how she saw his action in cutting her off from him.

He wasn't there, and she remembered he would be at the directors' meeting. A note on her desk confirmed that fact and a string of messages kept her busy for the next few hours.

He'd have seen it as the 'right' thing to do, she realised, when she allowed herself to think about the new revelations. Bathing himself in a rosy glow of nobility while he broke her heart! The anger seethed and burnt within her, but she had to push it back—to think about work, not Jake.

Impossible!

She did what she could, but the rage persisted, and when he opened the door, walked through it and smiled hesitantly at her, it was ready to erupt.

'I'm sorry, Katy, but we didn't have time to discuss the new unit.'

'Didn't have time!' The banked fires blew upward in a cataclysm of flame. 'No doubt there were far more important things to discuss! Well, I wouldn't want you putting yourself out for me—or for the people I feel are important. It's what you think that must come first— your perception of what's important and what isn't!'

She was nearly crying with rage, but the stunned look on Jake's face brought its own satisfaction.

'I'm going to lunch!' she added, grabbing her handbag and storming past his immobile figure and out the door.

He caught up with her as she waited, toe tapping in seething impatience, for the elevator.

'Would you mind explaining what that little outburst was all about?' he asked, speaking in a breathy undertone that whistled out through gritted teeth.

'No!' she snapped. 'Why should I? Since when did anything I think matter to you?'

'That's nonsense, Katy!' he argued, loudly enough for the little group of hopeful passengers to hear. 'Do you think I'd have disrupted my life like this if what you thought and felt didn't still matter to me?'

The lift arrived and the doors slid open.

'It didn't matter what I thought six years ago,' she flung at him, heedless of the onlookers. She plunged into the compartment as his pager sounded again. He began to follow her, then turned away to answer the call.

CHAPTER NINE

KATY headed for the crèche, intending to collect Julia and take her across to the park to eat their lunch by the lake. She forced herself to relax, to put Jake and the past right out of her mind before she saw her daughter.

'She's asleep,' Nan greeted her. 'My fault, I suppose, I let her stay up a bit late last night to watch a video with my kids.'

As she left the building on her own Katy's disappointment was diverted by thoughts of how often 'sight' words were used in conversation. 'Look at this.' 'Watch me.' 'Do you see?' Although Julia followed television by listening to words and sound effects, even she talked about 'watching' it.

Katy reached the park and found a seat by the lake. The sun burned into her skin but she relished its warmth—hoping it might banish her inner coldness.

The enormity of what Jake had done made it too difficult to consider logically. Earlier she'd reacted with anger over something else—but now it blotted out all thought processes, so she ate her sandwiches and stared out over the water.

The office was deserted when she returned, but a messenger came down from Admin only minutes later with the typed notes of the department directors' meeting.

She flicked through the printed pages. Jake had obviously had a legitimate excuse for not raising the new unit—the entire meeting seemed to have been devoted to discussing ways and means of handling 'celebrity' patients.

She turned to the last page and saw a recommendation that new procedures be put in place. Among the suggestions was one for a public relations office to be set up, headed by a person experienced in dealing with the media. Katy liked the idea. It would take pressure off units already under siege because they were housing the 'celebrity'.

And an official bulletin would be released at a specific time each day—which might stop the press from camping outside the front entrance hoping for a lucky photograph or a snippet of gossip.

The list continued and Katy could see sense in all of it. Bigger hospitals might already have such precautions in place, but Mrs Carstairs had been Lake Shore North's first experience of a media feeding-frenzy. At least the powers-that-be had learned from the experience.

She worked through the afternoon, her disappointment about the new unit very real—but blunted by thoughts of Jake's diagnosis, by wondering what she would have done if their situation had been reversed.

A sick feeling in her stomach told her she should understand his actions, but that didn't make them acceptable.

With a conscious effort, she set aside all thoughts of Jake. Her last duty for the day was always pleasurable, a quick visit to the wards to collect roster sheets and discharged patient files, and check there were no problems requiring her attention.

The doors to 'A' were tightly closed, and she experienced a pang of disappointment that her plan wasn't being put into action immediately. Having the empty ward would have made it so much easier to rearrange beds and patients.

Helen greeted her in 'B'.

The ward looked different, and Helen explained they'd brought in extra beds from 'A', although they weren't in use.

'We decided we'd put any new arrivals in here, even if it meant being a bit crowded. I've nabbed the extra staff from 'A', so staffing's no problem. Rosa has enough on her plate with Mrs Carstairs in one of her birthing suites and the Asian mothers in the ward area. It's worked out well. In fact, like the women in my ward, they've been most unimpressed by the fuss she's making and have withdrawn into their own exclusive little group. I think Mrs Carstairs would have preferred a bit of awe and admiration from her fellow patients, but she's certainly not getting it from those.'

'But if she's in a suite she wouldn't see much of the other patients,' Katy objected.

'No?' Helen said, and smiled at her. 'Before the latest incident, she'd taken to parading up and down the ward, talking about ''my babies'' in a loud voice. Sometimes Mr Carstairs followed her, but Rosa put a stop to his accompanying her, saying it was violating the other women's right to privacy.'

Katy shook her head, unable to believe the excesses of their famous patient.

'I'm glad Rosa was firm,' she said. 'Another belief among some of these women is that the baby shouldn't see too many strangers early in his or her life.'

'That stems from common-sense, really,' Helen agreed. 'The more people in contact with the baby, the more chance of someone passing on an infection of some kind.'

'The more I read of their customs, the more sense it all makes to me—apart from not showering!' Katy replied. She smiled at Helen. 'And what about Mrs Carstairs's health? Was the surgery successful? Has it calmed things down a bit?' she asked.

'Go see for yourself,' Helen suggested.

'I suppose I'll have to,' Katy said reluctantly. She walked on down the corridor and into 'C'. A nurse she didn't know was at the station, so Katy introduced herself and asked for Rosa.

'She's ducked out for ten minutes,' the young woman explained. 'I think she's probably on the fire stairs letting out great howls of frustration. It's been one of those days!'

'More trouble?'

The girl smiled and shook her head.

'Actually, a lot of the fuss has died down, and Mrs Carstairs hasn't been feeling well enough to think of a new sensation, but Mrs Robinson definitely wants to breast feed and she's been having trouble expressing milk. Rosa has spent a lot of time with her, trying various breast pumps, but we suspect the milk's not coming in because she's getting more and more distressed about it.'

'And the baby was pre-term, remember. All the proper signals weren't in place in her body.'

'That's true,' the nurse agreed. 'Actually, there's someone from the pre-term births association in there with her now. She's always more cheerful after one of their visits.'

'If her visitor leaves, I'll pop in and see her before I go.' Katy collected the roster sheets and patient files, then walked on into the ward. Her Vietnamese friend had been discharged that morning. Katy had no fears for her—her sensible husband would look after her well while she 'did the month'.

The woman from Hong Kong beckoned her, and Katy walked across and sat down in her visitor's chair.

'This is an excellent idea,' she told Katy, 'putting we Asian mothers together.'

Again Katy was struck by the differences more than the similarities between the women. Mrs 'Hong Kong', as Katy thought of her, was wearing an embroidered silk negligée with what looked like a white angora wrap thrown around her shoulders to keep her warm. Gold jewellery shone against her pearly skin—fat rings with glowing diamonds, heavy linked chains on her wrist and slung around her neck.

'It means we can do things in the old way and talk about the customs of our ancestors, but you need a steam room—and arrangements should be made about placentas for those who wish to know it has been properly treated.'

Katy tried not to shudder. She knew some South-East Asian people believed the placenta should be salted and buried outside their home to ensure a safe and happy life for the child. She hadn't included any suggestions about this custom in her file on the new unit because she couldn't see how the hospital could legally regulate such unorthodox disposal of what constituted waste product.

She ignored that issue and began to explain that the hospital was hoping to set up a special unit.

'Eventually, we hope to be able to offer far more than just grouping the patients,' she said.

'But I can do it now,' the woman said. 'You tell me how much it will cost and I will fix it.'

Katy felt her jaw drop. Until that very moment she'd always regarded the expression as ludicrous, but she had felt her jaw definitely slacken, no doubt leaving her mouth agape with shock.

'It's more involved than money—' Katy began to explain, but the woman waved away her objections.

'Work it out!' she ordered in a crisp, peremptory tone. 'I am staying here until Wednesday; tell me by then.'

Katy mumbled something soothing, spoke briefly to the other women and departed. Mrs 'Hong Kong' was obviously used to getting her own way—but if she wanted to give some money to the hospital, it was up to Katy to work out how best they might spend it. Perhaps a steam room would be possible after all!

She'd spoken to Sue Gates several times during the day, so she bypassed the nursery—although she'd have liked to have checked on the Robinson baby, and sneaked a quick look at the quins!

Back in her office, she tried three firms listed in the Yellow Pages as supplying steam baths and saunas, but all were closed. It was too late to do any more today and Julia would be growing impatient. Although the crèche remained open until after evening visiting hours, and even provided an overnight service to staff on night shifts, Julia believed five o'clock was 'going home time' and tended to nag when Katy was late.

Perhaps the money would be better spent on a language programme of some kind, she thought, and then, as she took the lift back to ground level, decided that the staff all managed quite well with sign language and the interpreters' help.

She collected Julia and listened to her chatter on about her day, grateful to Mrs 'Hong Kong' because considering her suggestion helped keep thoughts of Jake at bay.

Until he loomed up on the path in front of them and was greeted with great delight by Julia!

She seized his hand and began to swing, but Katy's warning growl was enough to convince her that it wasn't a good idea.

Julia chattered to Jake and Katy let her take control. She certainly couldn't have carried on a normal conversation. Her anger at Jake was still storming through her blood, but his presence prompted so many other responses her body felt at war with itself. His appeal—for her at least—was like a force-field of electrical currents, zapping constantly at her skin, her nerves...

'So you'll come?' Julia finished.

Come where? Katy wondered wildly. Where were they going in the near future? Where had Julia invited him?

'It might not suit your mother,' Jake said quietly, glancing towards Katy with a strange expression on her face.

She frowned, trying to think whether she'd promised Julia they'd go somewhere special, then her daughter answered for her.

'Oh, Mum never minds another one for dinner. Marie often comes, because it's on her way home from uni or she needs to study and her house is too noisy. But she won't come tonight because she's going to a rock concert.'

Ordinarily the information that the quiet, demure Marie was going to a rock concert would have diverted Katy, but she'd caught on to the question now.

Julia had invited Jake to *dinner*!

Tonight!

'Katy?'

So, he wasn't going to come unless she asked him—at least that was something.

'Please, Mum, please say yes!'

She looked down into the lovely sightless eyes and knew she couldn't disappoint the excited child.

'Of course you can come,' she said coolly, keeping any hint of welcome from her voice.

She had some chicken schnitzel—Julia's favourite food—in the freezer. She'd pull it out as soon as they reached the house. Her heart was thudding against her ribs, but she kept her mind on the practicalities of dinner. Thinking of chicken schnitzel stopped her thinking of electric currents.

He was the perfect guest.

He played with Julia while Katy fixed dinner, he cut Julia's schnitzel, and unobtrusively slid the pieces of chicken under her fork as she felt for them. He washed the dishes while Julia had her bath, then gave in to the child's pleas to read to her before she went to sleep.

Katy made a pot of coffee while he was upstairs. She didn't want him staying for coffee, but she had to do something to keep her hands and mind occupied. He had, as she'd suspected he would, invaded her house like an invisible fog—taking possession of its atmosphere with effortless ease.

If she closed her eyes, she could see him sitting on the floor, guiding Julia's hands as she fitted blocks together, pushing toys within reach so she didn't have to scramble for them. And as her heart ached for what might have been she forgot the past and felt her rage beginning to dissolve, washed away by the memory of a child's joyous laughter.

'She's waiting for her goodnight kiss.'

Jake's voice startled her out of her dreams.

'I'll go straight up,' she said, and hurried past him.

She realised—too late?—that the anger had been a barrier, some slight protection against his magnetic appeal.

'So, Katy?'

The words greeted her as she came cautiously down the stairs. He was sitting in the living room, his coffee poured and the cup clasped in his lean, tanned fingers.

'So what, Jake?' she muttered.

'So what was all that fury about this morning?' he said, his voice calm but implacable.

Fortunately she felt a flicker of the heat and fury return, and she procrastinated—hoping the flicker would strengthen into flame. She poured herself a cup of coffee, then sat down opposite him. Her house—quite adequate for two—seemed smaller now, and the sitting room felt more like a closet than the spacious room she'd once thought it.

'It was about something you said to me last week. "I had my reasons", you said, Jake.' She tried to listen to her voice, to see if she sounded as calm as she was pretending to be, but subtle nuances were beyond her. 'I saw your hospital records this morning.'

'Hospital records are confidential, Katy.'

His quiet, slightly reproving tone broke through her thin veneer of control.

'So report me and have me sacked,' she raged. 'What "reasons" did you have, Jake? That you were going to be crippled? What kind of a person did you think me, that you could possibly decide I'd be upset by that?

'I loved you, Jake—loved you so much it almost hurt to breathe—and you put me through hell because of your stupid pride. Because that's all it was, you know! You couldn't bear to think of yourself as less than perfect. You couldn't cope with me seeing you that way. I didn't hate you then—I couldn't—but I hate you now, Jake, hate to think you thought so little of me you could cut me off the way you did.'

Her fingers were shaking so much the hot coffee slopped over them. She reached out and put the cup down, feeling in her pocket for a handkerchief, blinking furiously to keep her tears from falling.

'It wasn't pride, Katy.'

He spoke into a silence that had seemed so complete she might have been alone.

'It was a lot of things but it wasn't that.'

She'd found her handkerchief and wiped her fingers. She blew her nose, then sniffed back a few more tears. She wanted rage, not tears!

'Well, don't stop there!' she snorted. 'What was it if it wasn't pride?'

He set his cup down carefully on the side table, then leaned forward. He was close enough to touch if she reached out. She pushed her body back into the chair—denying the urge!

'It was you,' he said softly. 'You and your damned independence! Honestly, Katy, you were the most stubbornly independent person I had ever met. You refused help from your friends, from people like Ben Logan, who would have done anything for you, and, most of all, you refused help from me—someone you supposedly loved!'

He looked up and she saw pain and grief in his eyes—recognising it because she'd seen it in her own eyes so often.

'So how do you think I felt when they said I'd probably never walk again? How do you think I felt when I realised I was going to be dependent on someone for the rest of my life—and, if we stayed together, dependent

on the world's most independent person? It was great
stuff, Katy, believe me!'

His voice was hoarse with the memories of that time
and she could hear the pain he must have felt.

'But I wouldn't have cared,' she yelled at him. 'Don't
you understand that? Didn't it enter your thick skull that
I loved *you*? Not an outer shell which could or couldn't
walk, but the person inside that shell—the bit of you
that laughed and cried and argued and helped me with
my studies and held me when things got too much to
handle. You could have kept doing all those things with
legs that didn't work.'

'I know you wouldn't have cared, Katy,' he said
gruffly. 'That was the problem. You'd have kept loving
me and bullied me to get better and taken me up as yet
another burden on your slim shoulders. But I cared too
much to let you do that. I loved you too much to diminish you that way, to have you give up your studies
to look after me, give up your dreams...'

His voice faded, then he added, 'But you did that anyway,' in a tight, hard voice, and leaned back in the chair,
as if saying the words had drained the last remnants of
his strength.

Katy could see his reasoning, could almost hear the
things he'd left unsaid. Caring for a paraplegic was
costly. She'd have had to accept hand-outs from his family, and her pride, not his, would have been ravaged in
the process.

'But we'd have made it,' she argued. 'We'd have
worked our way through it all.'

'Would we?' he asked.

She shook her head. No one could say for certain.
She'd seen so many relationships break down and die
when too much outside pressure was brought to bear,

and the pressures both she and Jake would have had to endure would have been enormous.

'You could have given me the choice!' she muttered, the old wrong not righted, the old pain still tender to the touch.

'I couldn't give you the choice,' he replied. 'You know how you'd have chosen. And I didn't want your love to turn to pity, our passion to die because I was a "duty". You'd have grown to resent me, to remember I went into that race against your wishes—wildly and recklessly brought the accident on myself! I couldn't take the risk—I couldn't give up what last shreds of self-respect I had. I couldn't let myself become dependent on you!'

His voice deepened with the strength of half-forgotten convictions, then softened as he continued, 'You, of all people, should understand, Katy. Would you have let me care for you if the positions had been reversed?'

Probably not, she thought, remembering she'd considered that question earlier today. But she wasn't going to admit it. The positions hadn't been reversed.

'You're walking now!' she pointed out, knowing he would understand all the things she hadn't said.

He bowed his head, and she saw his chest rise as he drew in a deep breath, then heard the sigh of its release.

'My parents flew me home from here. They called in more specialists and refused to accept the doctors' verdict—'

'You parents, Jake? Not you?' she interrupted, not willing to believe he'd been a passive patient.

'My parents,' he confirmed. 'I didn't care what happened to me, Katy. I'd lost you, lost my strength and nearly lost my mind! I'd lost too much to care about anything—and I was only too aware that the whole

blighted mess could have been avoided if I'd had one
shred of common-sense, so I had a load of guilt to bear
as well.'

'Go on,' she told him, feeling in her heart the deep
agony of regret which must have haunted him.

'They took me to America—to a specialist in the
United States. I went through barrages of tests again and
he decided it wasn't my back but my hip.'

'Weren't both legs paralysed?' Katy asked, drawn into
the medical aspect of the problem in spite of herself.

'They were, but this doctor decided it was sympathetic
paralysis in the right leg. He operated and released pressure on the sciatic nerve caused by the way the pelvic
bones had knitted together and he did a nerve repair of
a kind that hadn't then been tackled in Australia. It still
took time—two years before I was walking properly—
but—'

'And it didn't occur to you even then to write and
say, "I'm better, Katy". To tell me how you'd felt and
why you'd acted as you did. You had to wait another
four years, then smash your way back into my life—into
my house...' She was crying now in earnest, the tears
rolling down her face faster than she could wipe them
away. She bent her head so he couldn't see how deeply
his story had affected her.

'I did write!'

Her head jerked upward and she peered at him
through the blurred veil of sorrow in her eyes.

'When?' she demanded, hope and despair jostling in
her heart.

'In December of that first year,' he said. 'I sent you
a Christmas card from America with snow and robins
on it, because we'd always laughed about Christmas
cards like that out here, when it was ninety degrees in

the shade. I told you what was happening—why I'd lied to you that day and sent back your letters when I thought all hope was gone.'

In December she'd been in hospital, a thousand miles from Lake Shore. She'd been admitted, sick and weak from the prolonged diarrhoea of Giardia, at the beginning of the month. The trouble she'd assumed was persistent morning sickness had finally been diagnosed and she'd been treated, but it had been too late to save Julia from the effects of placental insufficiency. She'd been born on Christmas Eve, six weeks before she was due.

'I didn't get a letter,' Katy whispered, trying not to consider what such a letter would have meant to her at that stage.

'I know. It was returned to sender.'

'I moved in August,' she told him. Moved south and found a small flatette that faced the morning sun and would be suitable for a baby.

'I wrote care of the university, care of the hospital,' he added, 'and I even wrote to your father. The university and hospital letters came back, but your father didn't reply.'

Katy wrapped her arms around her stomach. She felt physically sick, as if all the lost years, the unhappiness and regret, were churning inside her.

She'd stopped her degree course when she'd realised it would be very hard to nurse and raise the baby on her own. The irregular hours and roster system would make her time with the baby too erratic, and the demands of the job would be physically draining. She'd brushed up her secretarial skills and worked from home instead, typing students' assignments and theses until Julia was twelve months old.

'Katy?'

One word, but a thousand questions.

He stood up and moved to stand beside her, his fingers trailing lightly down her hair.

'Go home, Jake,' she pleaded. 'I need to think about all this.'

He was silent for a moment, then he bent and kissed her on the cheek.

'Take your time, Katy,' he murmured, touching his lips against her temple. 'It took me over six years to come to terms with it—you're entitled to all the time you want.'

Then he knelt so he could look into her face and his eyes proclaimed a love so blinding she had to look away.

'You're also entitled to send me away—to say, Thanks, but no thanks Jake. I'd understand that—I wouldn't like it, but I'd understand—because what I did to you must seem close to unforgivable, and it would have to be forgiven before we could begin to recapture what we had.'

She wanted him to kiss her—wanted it so badly she trembled with the force of her desire—yet she knew he wouldn't. The next move would be up to her, and she wasn't so lost in dreams of hope and love that she could make it yet.

'Please go,' she repeated, and watched him stand up, hesitate, then touch her lightly before he moved away. She heard him fiddle with the front doorknob and knew he was setting it to lock behind him.

'Goodnight, Katy,' he called, then the door closed and she was alone with ghosts and images and reasonable-sounding if emotive explanations.

His story rang true—the tragedy of it all lying in the letters he'd written when she'd moved on into a different phase of her life and her whole being had been concentrated on her child—not forwarding addresses!

It had been deliberate, not leaving her new address when she'd shifted, not telling the hospital because she hadn't wanted to be found. She had cut herself off from all their acquaintances, at first to avoid their sympathy over Jake's accident and desertion, then to hide her pregnancy.

She'd moved away from Lake Shore, seeking anonymity in a bigger city further south, then returned when Julia was two and she'd heard of a special programme for sight-impaired children at Lake Shore North.

By the time she'd returned the programme had closed through lack of funds, but Katy had decided it was so good to be home she had found a job at the hospital and stayed.

So, Katy?

Her head repeated his words, but she couldn't make it think logically. It kept reminding her that what had happened once could happen again.

Another accident? desire argued sardonically.

Improbable!

But could some other change of direction provide a similar excuse for him to turn away?

She felt his parting touch as clearly as if his fingers still lingered on her skin, and recalled the shaft of longing that had pierced her at his soft caress. Her body ached for him in a way she would have thought impossible a week ago, yet she couldn't take that next step—that decision which would alter all their lives.

The phone rang while she was still sitting in the chair. She knew it was Jake and hesitated before reaching out to prevent the noise waking Julia.

'I know I said I'd let you think, but I need to know one thing.'

She didn't ask him what—couldn't speak for the joy fluttering in her throat, the joy just hearing his voice had set free.

'There's no other man, is there, Katy?' he demanded. 'I found it hard to believe you were still working so hard—' He broke off and she heard a husky mutter. 'Who am I kidding? I told myself there couldn't be— that my instinct about your reaction to me couldn't be that far out! And if that makes me sound conceited, I'm sorry—I don't mean it that way. It's a belonging kind of thing, Katy, a knowledge that comes from deep within that you and I are meant to be together.'

He paused, but she was too unexpectedly moved by his words to reply.

'Of course, I had other clues. Julia talked about her babysitter but never of her father. So tell me, Katy, make it definite. There's no one important in your life, no one you care about now, at the moment?'

She shook her head.

Only you, was the answer. There's only ever been you, she could have said. But she wasn't ready to tell him that yet, so she whispered her reply.

'There's no one else, Jake.' And she was about to hang up when he spoke again.

'And the flowers? And the ''John'' Jenny mentioned?'

He's jealous, she thought with an unfamiliar feeling of joy. Should she tease him?

She smiled to herself.

Not Jake! She'd never been able to hurt Jake, any more than she'd been able to hate him.

'The flowers were a thank-you from a support group I led for some years and John was a friend who never became more than that,' she told him, and heard his sigh of relief.

'For what it's worth, I love you, Katy,' he said quietly, and it was he who disconnected the call.

CHAPTER TEN

JULIA woke Katy in the morning. She was still dressed, still sitting in the armchair.

'You haven't been to bed,' her daughter accused.

'I must have fallen asleep in the chair,' she muttered, and made a joke of her silliness. But it was hard to laugh when her emotions were in tatters and her body ached from a cramped, uneasy sleep.

Another working day! She put out Julia's clothes, pleased the little girl insisted on dressing herself, then hurried into the shower. Warm water cascaded over her, so refreshing she tilted her head to let it flow over her hair as well. If she towelled it off it would be nearly dry by the time she'd walked to work.

She poured shampoo into her hand and lathered it into rich suds. Memories of Jake intruded. Jake washing her hair under the shower, letting the lather run all over her body—the lather and his hands...

'I'm ready for breakfast,' Julia called.

Julia? How would she adapt to another person in her life? Not another person—a father! She liked Jake well enough, but she was too young to understand what had happened between her parents. Would she hold his earlier desertion against him?

Katy dried herself and wrapped a towel around her wet hair. She dressed for work, then fixed breakfast for them both, eating hers at the kitchen bench while she made their sandwiches for lunch.

'Will Dr Cartwright come tonight?' Julia asked.

'I don't think so, pet,' Katy replied, and then she told herself the decision might be easier if she saw more of him outside working hours, and her heart missed a beat as she amended her reply to, 'Maybe!'

She left Julia playing downstairs while she combed out her hair and skimmed a sun-screening moisturiser across her face. She added a touch of green shadow above her eyes and emphasised her lips with a soft coral-pink lipstick. Her hair was damp, and she fluffed it out around her shoulders. She would brush it and confine it with a ribbon when she reached the crèche.

'Let's go, kid,' she called to Julia as she hurried down the stairs. She picked up Julia's backpack and her own handbag and they were ready to tackle another day.

'Dr Cartwright's waiting for us,' Julia announced when they reached the park.

This time Katy wasn't surprised by Julia's percipience. Knowing Jake, she'd guessed he would be here. He might say it was up to her to make the next move, but he'd never been one to stand back and let destiny run its course.

Well, not if he could give it a little nudge in the direction he had chosen!

They walked beside the lake, its placid surface a pale silver-blue reflection of the morning sky. Julia chatted companionably to Jake, and Katy was reminded of the 'X' in the equation. It would be so easy to give in to the love Jake professed, but at what stage in the proceedings did she introduce the subject of Julia?

Before they made love again?

Directly after, when he'd be relaxed and loving and—hopefully—understanding?

And what would she say? By the way, you have a daughter...

Her stomach flipped at the thought.

'You seem preoccupied this morning?' His voice slid into her consciousness and she turned to see his eyes gleaming with delight. He was so certain he had won, so sure she still returned the love he claimed had lived on in his heart.

Which she did!

She turned away without answering. She'd responded to his kisses, she'd admitted there was no other man in her life—it must seem so simple from his side.

They said goodbye to Julia at the crèche and Katy took Jake through the maze of corridors leading to the main lobby. He walked beside her, close, but not touching her, yet she could feel his presence as vividly as if they were standing naked together. Perhaps the mythical man in her life *had* been a protective barrier for her, or had Jake held back the full force of his attractiveness when he'd thought she was involved with someone else?

The feeling intensified when they crowded into the elevator and their clothes and skin brushed accidentally. By the time they exited into the fourth floor lobby Katy's nerves were twisted into a skein of torment, her body hungering for Jake's in a way she had never experienced before.

Six years' chastity, she reminded herself as she smiled and nodded to passing staff, hoping she looked more in control than she felt.

She made it to the office and slumped against the wall inside the door.

'You too?' Jake murmured gruffly, then he took her in his arms and held her close.

'Hell, Katy, what's happening to us?' he muttered, after they'd stood together for what seemed like hours. 'I felt so randy I could have thrown you down in the corridor in front of all those people, ripped the clothes off you and ravished you.'

'I wouldn't have fought you off,' Katy muttered, detaching herself shakily from his arms.

He ran his fingers through his hair and she saw the strain in his face give way to humour. 'Willing victim, huh?' he teased, and flicked one finger against her cheek.

'Willing, but stupid,' Katy told him, crossing to her desk and sitting down so she could at least pretend to be working.

'Stupid?'

She looked up at him.

'We're rushing into this, Jake,' she said. 'Going far too fast because of some hormonal thing that's battering at both of us.'

'Perhaps we'll think more clearly once we've given in to it,' he mocked, stepping very deliberately towards her. 'But I agree we should attempt to at least get through the day before weakening.'

He was standing on the far side of the desk and it was as if invisible threads bound her skin to his, tugging her towards him.

'I—I think that would be best,' she stuttered, wishing she felt more confident that getting through the day was possible.

He crossed to his chair and sat down, reaching out for his phone. She was thankful he'd begun to concentrate on work. Her phone rang and Katy seized it gratefully, hoping a sensible conversation would dispel images of the time she and Jake had made love on a desk—

'Hello!' she answered, dragging her mind back to the present.

'Are you on the pill, Katy?' a voice murmured in her ear.

She turned towards him and saw him smiling at her. She could feel heat colouring her cheeks, flowing through the most hidden parts of her body.

She tried to answer, but no words came, so she shook her head, remembered she hadn't tied her hair back tidily, stared at her brass pelvis, then dropped the receiver back onto its cradle.

Her hands were shaking—in fact her whole body was shaking! She rather suspected her mind was in similar turmoil, or had given up functioning. Through a haze of inconvenient emotion, she heard Jake's pager buzz, then he was on his feet, touching her lightly on the shoulder, and disappearing through the door.

He'd told her where he was going, but she hadn't made sense of the words—her usual cool efficiency and composure destroyed by a libidinous excitement.

She pulled out her diary and considered the day. No ward meeting—thank goodness! A note about steam rooms and saunas reminded her of the patient's offer. Doing something different might distract her, so she'd start there.

By lunchtime she had tackled all her regular jobs, and also had a list of three different portable units they could use within the hospital building. She'd checked with the hospital electrician and plumber to make certain the units could be installed safely and had quotes for the installation. The morning had gone more smoothly, she realised, because Jake had not reappeared.

Pleased with her efficiency, she decided to take a full hour for lunch. She collected Julia from the crèche, and walked with her to the lake. She deliberately blotted all thoughts of Jake from her mind while she enjoyed the time alone with her daughter. Jake might be impatient with destiny, but she'd gone beyond rational thought and was content to let fate take its course—for a while, at least.

When she returned Julia to Nan's care, she remembered another decision she'd taken and asked Nan to make arrangements to have Julia assessed. If it was done within the familiar preschool environment, her daughter would be more relaxed.

And if her daughter proved particularly gifted?

She shook her head, reluctant to confront that question. In fact, she half hoped the tests would show her daughter within the 'normal' range—whatever that might be!

A note on her desk told her Jake was in Outpatients if she needed him, but he'd be off duty by six and would like to take her and Julia out to dinner. 'I can borrow a car so be ready by six-thirty,' he'd written, and she could hear the peremptory tone he'd have used if he'd spoken the words to her.

Was dining with him—even with Julia as a safety valve—letting destiny carry her too far?

Probably!

But after the way she'd reacted to him this morning, destiny had already carried her past the point of no return.

She told herself that making love need not affect the choices she must make, although her heart knew a physical reunion could alter everything.

They went to dinner with him, Julia delighting in Jake's vivid description of the classy restaurant. Closing her eyes and listening to his words, Katy could see the sparkle of candlelight reflected off the silver cutlery, the drop of water on the rose petal in the silver bud vase on the table. She could feel the crispness of the linen napkins, and smell the rich medley of perfume and aftershave in the air around them.

'You asleep?' Jake murmured, and his fingers touched her thigh, electrifying her nerve-endings and starting a quiver of unfamiliar delight through her body.

'I often try to "see" it as Julia does,' she explained, opening her eyes to see the blazing message of desire he'd hidden behind the laconic words.

She knew her eyes were answering, but she'd known where this evening would end from the moment they'd left Julia at the crèche this morning. She just hadn't wanted to admit it—even to herself.

Somehow, she survived the meal. She was sure it had been delicious, but couldn't remember what she'd eaten. She knew Julia had kept the conversation going and hoped her daughter hadn't been too brash or cheeky. She'd responded—appropriately, she hoped—when someone spoke, and smiled a lot, for the conversations she had taken in had been amusingly different.

But destiny was sweeping her along—a leaf in a tide-tugged stream.

'Okay, we'd better take your mother home,' Jake said. 'I know she looks as if she's here, but she isn't with us.'

'Perhaps she's asleep,' Julia suggested, giggling with delight at the thought of a mother who'd slept through dinner.

'Perhaps she should have been,' Jake murmured in Katy's ear as he took her elbow and helped her up from her chair.

It was like waiting for exam results, Katy decided. A stomach-wrenching mixture of anticipation and dread. She made an effort to be sociable as they drove home, but it was hard to pretend it was a normal outing.

Julia fell asleep in the car, half woke as Jake carried her inside, then went straight back to sleep when Katy had undressed her, slid a nightdress over her head and tucked her into bed.

'Coffee?' Jake suggested when she made her way slowly back down the stairs.

She shook her head, too tense to speak, then stepped towards him as he came to meet her, his arms outstretched, his face alight with messages of love.

For a while they simply stood, letting their bodies absorb the secret scent and texture of each other, then Jake bent to kiss her and the room spun wildly.

'Shall we go upstairs?' he whispered, stroking the words against her skin.

She was beyond replying but she let him guide her upward. He knew Julia's room, so guessed the other would be hers, opening the door and sweeping her into his arms to carry her over the threshold.

Her heart was banging against her ribs and her breath fluttered in her lungs. Jake dropped her on the bed and looked around, his eyes gleaming with delight.

'Single bed? How virginal, my love.'

He knelt above her and began to undo the buttons of her dress, pushing back the material, his fingers lingering on the lacy bra she had beneath it.

Back to the buttons, each one so slowly extricated from its hole. Her body trembled with the prolongation of desire, this teasing dalliance that was heightening her need and sharpening her desire.

'So slim! So pale!'

His hand trailed across her stomach, then lingered on the lacy scrap of material below it. Heat surged between her thighs—remembered heat, remembered pulses of desire.

She was no longer able to stay passive, to take the feasting of his eyes and teasing of his fingers without response. She reached up and drew him down so he lay across her body, and while they kissed her fingers slipped his buttons free and pushed his shirt aside so skin met skin and sensory delights could multiply and magnify.

The kiss deepened, drawing out her air, her heart, her soul. She heard her own capitulation in a whimper of hunger, a sighing cry of yearning. They scrabbled their clothes aside, hands urgent now, felt for each other's bodies, drawing closer and closer, arms straining, fingers biting into flesh, pressing together to try to ease the pain of the aeons they'd spent apart.

Katy felt the heat of Jake's body transmitted into hers, felt the aching sexual emptiness which only he could fill. She arched towards him, lifting her body to invite him to take it and make it his once more, to work the magic of that wondrous release when the earth stopped turning and only she and he existed in the universe.

He hesitated, then she felt him press against her, his fingers teasing her to readiness before he entered her body and thrust inside her, timing his movements so the sensations twined and twisted, rising higher and higher, until they levelled off into a kind of suspended wonderment and then, at the next stroke, peaked and flew her far away, tendrils of delight rippling through her body, strangling her with potent magic.

Jake's shuddering groan matched her cry of triumph and she held him as he slumped against her.

'I love you, Katy—please love me again!' he muttered, his lips pressed to her ear so she couldn't miss the words.

Her arms tightened around his back but she couldn't

speak—too full of joy and wonder to think beyond this instant.

Until his hands began to move across her skin, and nerves which should have said, Enough, roused themselves again.

This time it was a different seduction. The lure of a worshipper, the intense delight of being praised, with hands and lips smoothing at her skin, teasing and tormenting, suckling at her breast, sliding up her thighs, fuelling the fires of her passion until she joined the game herself and, touch for touch, brought him to full arousal, then carefully raised the stakes a little higher, finding the protection he'd brought along and sliding it on while he groaned and threatened all manner of kinky punishment. Then she moved to sit astride him and watched his face as she made love to him.

'This bed is impossible,' he said, a long time later.

'It's fine for one,' Katy pointed out. Some vestiges of sanity were returning and she was faced—again—with the two great mountainous subjects still unresolved between them.

Would he go away again? was one. And Julia the other!

'I should go anyway,' Jake murmured, causing a momentary heart-stoppage with words that echoed her fears. 'Julia might not be ready to find me in the house at breakfast time!'

'We've got to talk,' Katy muttered, but he silenced her with a kiss.

'Isn't this better than talking?' he teased, and she found it was.

She must have fallen asleep, because she woke at dawn to find him gone. Her body was heavy with the aftermath of love, and pleasurably tender in parts. She sighed and rolled over, intending to go back to sleep for another hour, but her conscience reminded her that things were far from resolved between them, so she sat up in bed and worried for an hour instead.

He kissed her when she walked into the office and his hands flowed over her, as if to mark her with an invisible brand.

Mine! they said, and she would have revelled in the touch, but the problem of Julia was looming larger and larger.

'I'm on call tonight, but I could borrow the car again, then come to your place and be back at the hospital within minutes if I'm needed.'

She knew he was trying to arrange things now because who knew what emergency would arise to keep them apart for the rest of the day? But this headlong rush into a renewed relationship increased her uneasiness and she pulled away from him, flustered and embarrassed—and too intoxicated by his presence to think straight.

'It will be okay,' he assured her, as if he could feel her doubts and confusion. 'I know you must be concerned about Julia, you must have doubts about the future, but—' He caught her in his arms again and tilted her chin so she had to look up into his face. 'You can't deny what we do have going for us, Katy, or tell me you don't believe in my love for you.'

He kissed her again—a gentle, sweet, non-sexy kind of kiss that still lit fires beneath her skin. She was about to kiss him back when there was a tap on the door and Helen walked in. They sprang apart, too late to hide their closeness but quickly enough to underline their guilt.

'Well, well!' Helen remarked to the air between them.

'That was quick work. I can come back later, if you like.'

Katy stumbled into denials, explanations and excuses, but Jake reached out and slid his hand across her mouth.

'We're old friends,' he said smoothly. 'Now, did you want me or Katy?'

'Both, as it happens,' Helen told him, her eyes gleaming as she absorbed the value of this new bit of hospital gossip. 'I was bringing these requisition forms to Katy, so I became the message girl. Dr Anderson would like you to meet him in the lobby, Dr Cartwright, and Rosa wants to speak to Katy.'

Katy took the sheaf of papers and dropped them on her desk. She was mortified by her unprofessional behaviour—and by being caught in Jake's arms. She followed Jake and Helen from the room, trying to regain the enthusiastic efficiency with which she usually approached her work.

'Mrs Li would like to speak to you,' Rosa told her, using Mrs 'Hong Kong's' real name. 'I said you couldn't make the decision about the new unit, but she seemed to think she might be able to bring influence to bear somewhere if you explained your idea.'

Katy groaned. She was already behind in her morning's work—thanks to Jake's insidious influence—and now another hour or two would be lost as she set out the details of her plan for Mrs Li.

Still, if the woman was willing to make a donation, and if she did have influence in the district, maybe...

She entered the ward and took the visitor's chair beside the new mother.

'I've found out about steam baths and saunas,' she

began, and went on to explain how things stood at the moment.

'Yes! Now you have explained, I understand how important it is to do this properly,' Mrs Li said later. 'Especially in the antenatal stages. Perhaps I could organise some friends to talk to other Asian mothers and undertake some research into the various customs. We could begin with the women I have met in here. Younger Auntie knows much, and my new Cambodian friend has a book printed in her country on the ways of childbirth and confinement. Leave it to me!' she ordered, with a wide sweep of the jewelled hands. 'First I get the information, then I pay someone to collate it all. We will get your unit started without the hospital permission.'

Katy felt she'd been dismissed. She thanked the woman and left the ward. She'd meant to talk to Jake about this offer of financial help, but somehow it had slipped her mind last night!

'I wonder why?' she muttered to herself.

'Tonight?' Jake asked as they passed in the corridor a little later.

Katy shook her head, then nodded, not knowing what she wanted to do. He'd said he'd give her time, but she knew she couldn't bring herself to demand it. Already she was thinking about this evening, about their lying together in her narrow bed as soon as Julia had gone to sleep!

Julia! The still-unknown! Panic skittered in her heart and she forced it back, but in the end it was Julia who precipitated the confession. Julia, showing off to Jake later that evening, counting to one hundred, adding and subtracting, challenging him to give her harder sums.

'Not bad for a cheeky kid who's only—what?' he

said, taking her in his arms and tossing her gently into the air. 'Three and a half? Four?'

She was squealing with delight and so breathless she had difficulty answering.

'No, no, silly,' she squealed. 'I'm not a baby. I'm five—and this Christmas I'll be six.'

Katy heard the silence stiffen into something hard and awkward.

'Five!' Jake echoed. 'Six at Christmas!'

He didn't need his special gifts to do the sums, nor did Katy need a translator to tell her how he felt.

Across Julia's blonde head he looked at her, his eyes dark and hard with anger and disbelief.

He put Julia down with exaggerated care—bent and kissed her on the cheek.

'I'll see you soon, little one,' he said softly, then he turned and walked towards the door.

Katy held her breath and waited. Surely he'd turn back—say something! Anything!

She shivered in the warm night air and watched him fiddle with the catch, setting it to lock behind him.

She tried to call to him, but her lips weren't working, so she watched the door open, then close behind him, and she wondered if he'd cut her out of his life for a second time.

CHAPTER ELEVEN

JAKE didn't phone to say goodnight—although that didn't surprise Katy. Nor was he in the office when she arrived for work, and she wasn't certain if she was pleased or sorry. The strain was plucking at her nerves, making concentration difficult.

At ten he came through the door and glanced towards her as he said, 'I'd like you to sit in on this meeting, please, Katy.'

No smile, no blazing message of either love or desire in his blue eyes.

A strange, leaden feeling filled her chest, but she couldn't begin to guess what he might be thinking. He wouldn't give up Julia now he knew he had a child—but would Katy be included in the package?

Ron Spencer had followed Jake into the room, now Helen entered, and with her Stewart Anderson.

Jake settled them in chairs and Katy grabbed a note-pad from her desk and dragged her own chair across to join them. She didn't look at Jake but she knew every time he shifted in his chair, and her fingers remembered the shape and feel of the scars his accident had left on his body.

'I want to run through a few ideas I've been mulling over about the new unit and the care of mothers from South-East Asia,' he said crisply.

Katy dragged her mind away from thoughts of his body and tried to concentrate on what was being said.

'I know you don't see many of them, Stewart, as they're mostly public patients—'

'Don't you believe it,' Dr Anderson interjected. 'More and more of my patients are Asian women. In fact, I'm trying to learn basic Chinese at the moment, although I miss half the classes because I'm called out.'

Jake nodded.

Katy thought she could detect a greyness in his skin, as if he hadn't slept well. Work, or worry? she wondered, and felt a twinge of guilt that she should be adding personal concerns to his burden of responsibility at the hospital. I shouldn't have let him walk out like that! she thought. I should have made him stay and talk about what had happened.

But Julia had been awake, and he'd been hurt—upset...

'Good—you'll understand where I'm coming from,' Jake continued, and again Katy tried to focus on the present, not the past. 'Although the board hasn't yet approved a unit, as such, I've been wondering if we can't organise outpatient visits along the lines Katy's outline suggests. Most of the Asian women come on the same day as it is, so could we have a ''clinic'' approach, with a group session early in the day, then individual appointments later?'

'I could see Nan at the crèche and make certain she has a Chinese-speaking aide on duty on those days,' Helen suggested, 'so the women could leave their pre-school children there. The main reason women don't like to be away from home too long is because of shaky childcare arrangements.'

'Gran will mind the kids for two hours, but if you're any longer she gets upset!' Ron put in, and Katy smiled. He and his wife, a GP in a small practise near the hospital, had three children under five, so he understood the problems.

'That's a good idea, Helen,' Jake applauded, then he looked at Katy. 'What's the best way to tackle educating these women in our ways?' he asked, as a colleague not a lover—perhaps not even a friend. She recalled discussions she'd had with her Chinese friend about this subject.

'I think if we had leaflets printed in Chinese, Vietnamese and Cambodian for a start—explaining why women should see a doctor during their pregnancy, what each visit will entail, how to know when it's time to come to the hospital for the baby, what to bring and what will happen when they get here...'

'But they might find our ways so offensive they avoid us,' Jake argued. 'Hasn't that been the problem in the past?'

Katy nodded, but Helen answered for her.

'I think the leaflet should emphasise that this is how we, as Westerners, do it, but that every effort will be made to fit into the patient's way. It should point out that one of the reasons it's important for them to attend antenatal clinics is so we can find out their customs and how they would like things done.'

'You could be quite definite about it,' Dr Anderson said. 'Say something like, "It will be hard for us to do things your way if you don't help us learn the customs."'

Everyone nodded and Katy felt a little surge of excitement break through the lump of dread and worry in her chest. Perhaps it was time to mention Mrs Li.

'A patient in Rosa's ward at the moment is willing to help financially.' She explained about the sauna and steam baths. 'I think a sauna might be better, because it comes as a unit that can be fitted into a shower stall and the patient can sit in it and cleanse herself in the traditional way.'

She went on to tell them of Mrs Li's idea of researching the customs and collating them into a form which could be used for staff training. Her concern over the mess in her personal life was pushed aside as she concentrated on work.

'That's great,' Ron said. 'Well done, Katy! And when's the sauna being installed? I've often thought I could do with a steam clean after a big night out!'

Katy smiled at him.

'It's the installation that might be a problem,' she said. 'Since Helen, Jenny and Rosa have managed to group the Asian women together in 'C' this week, I've been wondering if the unit has to be a special space. Couldn't it be more of a concept?'

'I've been thinking that myself, Katy.' Jake glanced her way but didn't really look at her. No half-smile, no secret gleam of light in his eyes! 'Do we have to make, say, 'A' Ward, the ward for Asian women? Or could we simply keep them together in whatever ward has the beds. That way they're not completely isolated from the other mothers and the cross-cultural influence can go both ways.'

'That's what I'd thought,' Katy agreed. 'And with a more flexible approach it might be better to get a steam bath which can be relocated to whatever set of ward bathrooms the women are using.'

Helen muttered about extra work, but Jake silenced her.

'Would they really mind walking a little further to have their sauna?' he asked. 'I've been thinking about Jenny's suggestion for more birthing suites. I have to study the figures, but I've noticed the three wards aren't used to full capacity, so we could probably fit two birthing suites and a special sauna room into 'A', which would solve the problem of shifting things around.'

There was a moment's silence while they pictured the changes.

'It could work,' Helen said, 'because the suites are large enough to take two beds. If we did get busy, we could use them as double rooms.'

'So we begin by getting information printed?' Jake asked. Helen and the two men agreed, Helen offering to adapt and extend their English-language leaflet to include all the necessary information before passing it on to the interpreting service for translation.

'Why wasn't all this done earlier, Katy?' Jake asked as the others left the room.

She was pleased his mind was still fixed firmly on a work-related topic, because she wasn't ready for a confrontation yet.

'The influx of Asian migrants is fairly recent,' she explained. 'Two years ago a new manufacturing business was set up on the outskirts of the city. It makes metal fittings for heavy machinery. A number of Asian families moved in as both men and women were needed for jobs on the assembly line. Then a big food chain set up a distribution centre here, and there were more jobs available, and last year a computer software business began operation—more jobs, but this time for skilled workers and technicians. The owners are a group of Australian-Chinese businessmen who decided the area had more growth potential.'

'So the immigrant population has mushroomed in a very short time,' he said, crossing to the window and staring out towards the lake.

'And we've been slow to catch on to the change,' she admitted. 'A big organisation like this, that's doing well enough, doesn't change direction quickly.'

'Unless someone stirs them into action,' he said. 'A fighter like you!'

He turned back towards her and she knew the moment had arrived.

'Is Julia my child, Katy?' he asked.

She frowned at him. She'd expected many questions, but not that one.

'Of—of course she is,' she stuttered. 'You worked out the dates! What did you think? That I'd been having an affair with someone else while we were lovers? Is that why you were so upset last night? Is that why you walked out? How could you possibly believe such a thing?'

Her anxiety had peaked and she let the words lash out at him, hoping they were hurting him as much as his shock assumption had hurt her.

'You weren't pregnant,' he pointed out. 'We did the test. You were sick, but you said the other day that it was Giardia...'

The words faltered. She couldn't see his eyes but knew they'd be dark with the pain and confusion she could hear in his voice.

'We made love that morning, before you left, if you remember...'

Now her own voice stuck, because it had been a strained, sad-angry kind of mating and she'd always felt children should be conceived in love.

She tried again, remembering the theory she'd worked out—months after the accident—when she'd begun to suspect there were two changes occurring in her body, not just one sickness that came and went, draining her energy and dulling the pain of Jake's loss.

'I'd been sick on and off for weeks. It must have affected the barrier effect of the pill I was taking.'

Her body was stiff with tension. She didn't want to handle this alone, to remember her despair and fear, and the dragging debility of an undiagnosed condition. She looked at Jake but he'd turned back towards the window, heedless of her silent calls for him to hold her in his arms.

'You should have told me!' he said harshly. 'You must have known it would have changed things.'

'Made you love me again when you'd said it was all over, Jake? I didn't think so!'

Why was she hesitating? Why hold back because the truth might hurt?

Because she loved him!

'It was my right to know!' he objected, and she knew she'd have to tell him, however much it hurt.

'I did write,' she said bluntly. 'Twice! You sent the letters back!'

She saw his head bend to touch the window and his shoulders slump forward.

'Oh, Katy!' he said, the words a groan dredged up from the depths of his being. 'Oh, Katy, what did I do to you? To Julia—my own child?'

She crossed the room, needing to touch him, to offer the physical support she'd wanted earlier, but the phone rang and she remembered they were both at work, and a ten-minute lull—though it had seemed like an hour—was a rare occurrence in their work-day lives.

'You're needed in Theatre,' she told him, her heart contracting at the ravaged look of grief on his face.

'Can you forgive me? Is it possible we can start again?' he asked.

'Let's talk about it later, Jake,' she said quietly, still conscious of the hurt his doubt had dealt her.

She turned back to her desk and went on with her work, but even the excitement of knowing they could begin to put her plans for the Asian patients into action failed to stop the nagging uneasiness after their unresolved conversation.

She didn't want Jake feeling guilty about the past. She wanted him making positive moves towards the future—helping her think through the implications for Julia, discussing how best they should handle it.

Her heart told her the future would include Jake, that they would be a family, but there was one last fence to jump and she couldn't do that on her own.

She didn't see him again that morning, but he phoned at two to say he would be finishing early and could he walk them home.

'Of course,' she said, because the messages of pain had diminished in his tone and the sound of love was softening every consonant.

'If I don't get back to the office I'll meet you at the crèche—five-thirty at the latest.'

He paused, and she wondered where he was and who was listening, for his *I love you, Katy* seemed to echo through the silence—unsaid, but deeply felt.

'I love you, too,' she murmured, pleased to have the words said at last.

She thought she heard him smile before the click told her they'd been disconnected, and the afternoon flew by as she anticipated seeing him again.

'Let's sit a while and talk about the swans,' he said, when they'd walked beside the lake in a silence broken only by Julia's demands and chatter.

They reached a bench overlooking the lake and Jake took Katy's hand and held it, even after they were seated. Julia climbed confidently up and settled on the other side of Jake.

'You holding Mum's hand?' she asked suspiciously.

'I am,' Jake told her. 'That's what I want to talk to you about.'

'Is it love stuff?' Julia asked, and Katy blushed at the precocious tone.

'Very much so,' Jake replied, his voice edged with laughter. 'What do you know about ''love stuff''?'

There was silence while Julia considered the question.

'Nan's kids talk about it all the time,' she confided in the end.

'They're teenagers!' Katy added, by way of explanation.

'And I know about the swans,' Julia told him. 'They love each other.'

'They do,' Jake agreed, in a husky voice. 'What I want to tell you, Julia, is that I knew your Mum a long time ago and we were very much in love.'

'Did you live at Lake Shore then?' Julia asked, as if she needed to get the setting for this story straight.

'I did,' he told her, slipping an arm around her shoulders so her head rested against his chest. 'I came here to work at the General Hospital and your mum was the very first person I met! Oh, we had some fun!'

Katy found it hard to breathe. Jake was doing very well, so far, but how would he introduce himself as her father?

'We were going to get married, only then I did something very, very stupid and I hurt myself—'

Julia pushed away from him and turned towards the sound of his voice.

'You had an accident!' Julia shouted, anticipating the next part of the story. 'You're my father?' she cried. 'My really, truly father? Oh, Dr Cartwright, can I feel what you look like?'

Katy swallowed the lump of tears and watched through watery eyes as Julia scrambled onto Jake's knee and ran her tiny fingers over the planes and angles of his face. She could see the tears in his eyes, too, and feel his tension in the fingers biting into the flesh of her hand.

Then Julia sighed and relaxed against Jake's body, and his arm drew her against his chest and held her close. He turned to Katy, a thousand questions in his eyes, but she answered only one.

'I think she's got your IQ as well,' she said, and tried to smile.

A long time later, she stood with Jake beside Julia's bed and watched their daughter sleep.

'I have to thank you, Katy,' he said gruffly as they left the room and walked back down the stairs.

'Why?' she asked, heading for the couch where they could sit together. She felt drained by all the emotion of the last twenty-four hours, wanting just to relax and let the tumult in her world die down.

'For not turning her against me,' he said, sitting down beside her and kissing her gently on the cheek. 'What had you told her that she made the leap from accident to father?'

His hand found hers and he held it, lifting it to his lips and kissing her fingers one by one.

'I said you'd been so badly hurt you'd had to go away and learn to walk again.'

She looked at Jake and saw he understood now the depths of the pain she'd endured—understood she hadn't had the courage to cut him out of her life completely, and, most important of all, knew she'd never hated him!

He leant forward and kissed her on the lips.

'I didn't deserve your unselfish kind of love,' he muttered. 'I was too young and full of myself to realise how rare and beautiful it was!' He kissed her again, a silent pledge, then straightened up.

'So, she always thought I might come back?' he asked, and Katy frowned.

'I didn't want her thinking that,' she told him. 'In fact, I tried to make it sound as if you would have if you'd been able but it was impossible.'

'But you didn't let her hate me, Katy!' he said, his voice full of wonder and relief.

'How could I, Jake?' she asked, and this time she turned and kissed him, on the cheek. 'I couldn't have my daughter hating the only man I'd ever loved—ever would love, could love, will love!'

'Are you sure of that, my darling?' he murmured, taking her in his arms and looking down into her eyes. 'Quite, quite sure, my one and only best, best girl?'

She smiled and kissed him again, this time on the lips, then drew back for long enough to say, 'I'm certain!' before she let her lips find his and felt the blood flow swiftly through her veins, carrying sweet messages of love throughout her body.

JANICE KAISER

FAIR GAME

Dana Kirk is a rich and successful woman, but someone
wants to kill her and her teenage daughter. Who hates
her enough to terrorise this single mother? Detective
Mitchell Cross knows she needs help—
his help—to stay alive.

*"...enough plot twists and turns to delight
armchair sleuths"*—Publishers Weekly

1-55166-065-2
AVAILABLE FROM MARCH 1998

Catherine Coulter

Afterglow

Chalk-and-cheese lovers Chelsea Lattimer and
David Winter finally find happiness after a series
of disastrous relationships—thanks to their
match-making friends.

Afterglow is a wonderful romantic comedy from
New York Times bestselling author Catherine Coulter.

MIRA

1-55166-472-0
AVAILABLE FROM MARCH 1998

JOANN
ROSS

NO REGRETS

Three sisters torn apart by tragedy each choose a
different path—until fate and one man reunites them.
Only when tragedy strikes again can the surviving
sisters allow themselves to choose happiness—
if they dare pay the price.

"A steamy, fast-paced read."
—Publishers Weekly

1-55166-282-5
AVAILABLE FROM FEBRUARY 1998

HEATHER GRAHAM POZZESSERE

If looks could kill

Madison wasn't there when her mother was
murdered, but she *saw* it happen. Years later, a
killer is stalking women in Miami and Madison's
nightmare visions have returned. Can FBI agent
Kyle Montgomery catch the serial killer before
Madison becomes his next victim?

"...an incredible storyteller!"—LA Daily News